THE GEORGETTE HARVEY STORY
by
CAROL SPEED

IN MEMORY OF MARK EVERETT SPEED

Author of: Inside Black Hollywood

PROTEA PUBLISHING

Copyright 1989 – 2002 Carol Speed. All rights reserved.

The Georgette Harvey Story
by Carol Speed

First Edition Worldwide

ISBN 1-931768-68-4

Protea Publishing. USA
kaolink@msn.com
www.proteapublishing.com

Part I

St. Louis

Chapter 1
(1884 - 1904)

My grandmother was a slave. Mary Donaldson was her name. She knew the cruel lash of the whip. All the hardships of slavery, and the joy of being freed. Mary Donaldson was a great cook on a plantation somewhere in Mississippi. She glorified in having cooked a Christmas dinner for Robert E. Lee, "biggest leader and General" of the Confederate Army.

On December 31, 1884 in St. Louis - twenty-five years later, after Granny and Momma had settled - I was born squealing and yelling like a stuck pig. In fact I was screaming so loudly, I could be heard four doors away. Granny said, "Well, from them lungs, she'll never have consumption!" This caused great rejoicing, on account of my brother, Guy. He was two years my senior and epileptic. And then there I was, a robust, bouncing, healthy baby.

In those days women like Momma hardly had time to spare from their laundry work. Yet they needed to stay in bed the nine days required for recuperation. Having a baby was just a sort of thing to get over with quick as possible. But wise Granny, a midwife, made Momma stay in bed the full time.

Lucy Harvey, my mother, was a fine looking woman. She wasn't dark, but more the Indian type. In fact, she was of Indian extraction. Her grandfather's side being Apache Indians.

Momma had a great sense of humour. Sorrow never crushed her. She was always jolly, teaching us to sing all the time. She loved singing in the Trinity Baptist Church choir. Or singing anywhere, as a matter of fact. So after she began to work for the white people around St. Louis - for their teas and things - shortly after I was born, a white woman got interested in her voice. She wanted to send Momma abroad to study in places like France and Italy. However, Granny said "no." She'd never seen nothing like oceans. But she'd heard about them. And for the life of her, she just couldn't understand anybody ever crossing so much water and coming home. Yet even though Granny said no, Momma just kept right on singing happily. She loved singing so much. She wanted me to be a singer. But what she wanted, most of all for me, was to be a school teacher of music.

Jim Harvey, my father, was a drunkard. He and Momma used to quarrel all the time. After one really bad quarrel when I was about three months old, he tried to steal me. But Granny beat him over the head with a cast iron skillet. She hit him so hard, she almost killed him. After that he drank so heavy that Momma left him. I was about six months old then. All I knew regarding my father is from what I remember Momma telling me. It seems he was very fair skinned, tall, thin-featured, had dark brown curly hair, and was extremely handsome. His grandmother was an Irish woman.

After Momma left him, he was heard of no more until he died. That was when I was eighteen months old. She didn't wear no mourning for him. When anybody asked her why not, she exclaimed, "I wore nough mourning round my heart for Jim Harvey when he was living!" But she did love him. "I was crazy bout your father! And Lordie could that man sing. We really sung some beautiful music together." That's the one special thing I remember her saying.

From four to five years of age - about 1888 - my memory began working. I can distinctly remember one bright spring Sunday morning. Everybody had gone to church leaving me home. I wasn't feeling so good. I sat on the kitchen floor in the corner by the stove, just looking up at Momma's big cage of canaries. I'd always wanted to play with them. They sang so pretty and were such a beautiful yellow colour. Finally, I climbed up on a chair and opened the cage door. The birds flew about frantically. Then they crowded to the far corner of the cage. "I don't want to hurt you," I explained gently. "I just want to play with you." They all fluttered at once and flew out! I practically fell off the chair. What Momma wouldn't do to me! She'd beat me sure. She'd seem to thrash me every day the Lord sent anyway!

"Come back pretty birds…please, come back." They paid me no mind. They just sat around on the roof and trees and didn't move. I made bird noises, beeps and tweets but they didn't budge. Try as I might those damned canaries wouldn't come back.

Momma came in and immediately noticed the empty cage. She didn't say a thing - just gave me a steely glance. Then she put a little birdseed on the porch railing while she talked softly to the birds. They all slowly came back excepting three. Calmly she latched their door. The birds were so happy to be home again. They just flew around singing and singing. Momma said, "Georgie Harvey, sick or no sick, you're gonna get it!" And for a week, I had to eat standing up. I never touched those canaries again. I just wasn't interested anymore. All that I remember clearer than some things which happened to me last week. And it all happened over fifty years ago.

At that time we lived in the southeast section of St. Louis. It was a two-story frame house on West Jefferson Avenue, between Ohio and Choutoau Avenues. West Jefferson was only a block long. We and the downstairs people were the only colored folks in the vicinity.

We had two rooms upstairs for which we paid seven or eight dollars a month. Even that was hard to pay. Momma and Granny took in washing. Although, the amount of washing you pay three dollars for now could easily, in those days, be done for seventy-five cents. Momma and Granny did the landlord's washing as part payment on the rent. And even so, they still had to work day and night.

Everything was compared to today's prices much cheaper. Even butter was only ten or fifteen cents a pound. But it was seldom we had butter. It was one of the biggest luxuries we enjoyed. We always used giblet-gravy. Of course, we usually had plenty of that plus some. Momma and Granny worked for Mr. Seidl, the butcher. They plucked and cleaned chickens, getting all the giblets in return. That's the way we got most of our food. Sometimes Mr. Seidl threw in a roast. And when we had more than enough, Granny sent me to some of the other colored people with a pot of giblets. They were always welcome to them.

Granny and Momma also worked for Mr. Rose. He lived on the corner and owned the Dairy, Pork, and Slaughter House. The Roses had a great, big, black, iron pot in their backyard. Under this pot were immense logs of wood. And every late September when the leaves started turning orange, yellow, and reddish colours, you could find Granny stirring apple butter in that pot. She'd stand flat-footed on the dry golden grass using a long stick shaped like a flat ladle. So at Christmas time Mr. Rose always made us a present of a sugar-cured ham.

We usually had plenty to eat. Although, our two rooms were quite sparsely furnished. Mostly with only what had been discarded or given to us by people Granny and Momma worked for. The bed they both slept in was big and real mahogany. A little trundle bed, on the other side of the room, was where I slept with Brother Guy. There was also a walnut bureau with brass handles and three big dark chairs. One was stuffed, but the hard chairs were my favorites. In the center of the floor sat an elegant mahogany, marble-topped table that subsequently saved our lives. On the front room floor were mats which Granny sometimes wove at night. All our light came from one large and one small oil lamp.

There was no bathroom. For natural causes we had to go out into the yard, and at night we used the pot. However, the first thing the next morning, we carried the pot out. Contrary to most people's thinking, St. Louis is a very cold place at times. One time it was so cold (only two blocks from school) my fingers and toes were frost bitten. It must have been twenty-two degrees below zero!

To catch rain water for washing, Momma kept two tubs on the long porch. That porch was so long, it ran the entire length of our rooms. All other water had to be carried from the yard, where there was a hydrant. Even still we bathed winter and summer. Saturday, Tuesday, and Thursday nights always found us in the washtub scrubbing real hard with soap. Granny's own soap made from grease and lye.

Our clothes, also, came from people Momma worked for, but did I dress. I was the envy of all the kids on our block. I had some lovely dresses from a wealthy woman, Mrs. Aronstein. Her daughter, Thelma, was just my age. Sometimes Thelma's clothes were scarce used. I had twenty-six beautiful aprons, too. These aprons came from one family who had five girls. Momma made me wear them to school. In those days all girls wore aprons.

I was forever crazy about my feet and still am. My shoes, also, came from Thelma and the other girls. Yet somehow they always seem to fit. I had two pairs of patent leather shoes with cloth tops. If you even had one pair of shoes like those you were the "bee's knees." They were supposed to be my Sunday best. However, when I could I'd slip them on and wear them to school. Momma would thrash me, but I didn't care. I, also, had lots of hair ribbons and imitation gold bracelets. I sure was a nice looking kid in all my elegant finery. Everybody loved me, but I was a ring-tailed devil.

Coming home from Sunday school one day, my dearest playmate ran to meet me. Now I was rigged out with special brilliance in a white embroidered dress, red shoes with silver buckles, and a large white leghorn hat. Did I feel grand. I just stuck my nose in the air higher than a kite. Then proceeded to high-hat my little redheaded Irish friend. "I can't play with you, Irene Donavan, until you can afford a Sunday dress like mine!" She gave me one amazed look. She screamed! She howled! She ran to Momma! "Miss Harvey! Tutti won't play with me, cause I ain't got a dress like hers!"

"Is that so!" Momma grabbed me, dragged me in, undressed me, and shoved me in bed. This was too much. I almost cried my eyes out. That tattle-tale, Irene. I'd sure punish her. Finally, I cried myself to sleep. But when I was allowed out, I promptly beat my best friend up. Momma put me in bed again, but that didn't lessen my love for pretty clothes.

Chapter 2

In my mind's eye, I can still see Granny. Just as plain as day, as if I was about four or five. She wasn't a tall woman. And was what's called "the Guinea Type": very dark, smooth-featured with kinky hair. She was very straight standing. So determined about everything that she walked with a haughty carriage. She feared nothing, and people loved her. White people idolized her.

Although Granny didn't have time to visit anybody, because she had to stay home and work hard. The kitchen was forever full of folks visiting her. Where she was always bending over the washtub or shoving a heavy flat-iron, and singing her favourite spirituals:

> "I'm just agoin over Jordon!
> I'm just agoin over home!
> There's no dark clouds will hover
> Round me;
> I'm just agoin over home!"

She'd sing these type of songs over and again. Then one by one her friends would fall in with such a music...such a harmony that I was almost wafted into heaven. It was, however, a long dreary business washing and ironing. The weighty flat-irons had to be heated. The filthy clothes had to be boiled until they were white. This boiling took place in the ancient leaky boiler on the old slow-burning coal stove. Those dirty clothes would have to be stirred. Then they had to be beaten with a ancient broom handle, before they became white. That was a back-breaking job for a young woman - let alone an old woman.

The only amusement Granny ever had was those visits from her friends. They'd also been slaves. While I lay in bed with Guy, they all sat out in the kitchen talking and singing. They'd tell the most fascinating stories. My brother slept, but my ears stood wide open. I was a kid that loved hearing stories.

Granny related how when she was a slave, her mistress flogged her unmercifully. She was extremely cruel and did everything in her power to make Granny and the other slaves miserable. So Granny took some of her mistress's beautiful red hair from combings. Then put it in a bottle with some of her mistress's urine, along with nine new pins, and nine new needles. She then buried it at midnight during a certain time of the moon, putting it under the doorstep where her mistress had to cross in and out. At the end of nine days, the mistress went raving crazy and died!

This was Voodooism. Of course, Granny didn't really believe in any of it. Although, it seemed the only way slaves could fight back against wrongs. Yet when Granny made up her mind to escape, she decided not to use Voodoo. She wasn't afraid of being caught by her own white folks…the Gorillas was the only thing she truly worried about.

The Gorillas were the Ku Klux Klan of that day. They would catch escaping slaves, flog them brutally until their bodies ran red with blood, then sell them at auction as tamed slaves. In such transactions, a child was often torn away from the breast of its mother and never seen again. Momma was a babe in arms. This was the one thing Granny never wanted to lose…her child.

Granny was the cook for the family, and the slaves. So she knew most Southerners were particularly fond of biscuits. While one of the slaves from a nearby plantation kept Momma, Granny prepared supper - filling the biscuits full of croton oil. Then she got permission to go to a slave dance that was being held at a nearby plantation.

Supper was served around seven-thirty. While everybody was eating, Granny changed from her drab blue slouch-dress to her green print Sunday-go-to-meeting clothes. She set off. Not really knowing where she was going after she got to the neighboring plantation. She'd never been farther than that, but she did know…by talk at the "Big House"…the Union side wasn't very far away. Some sort of river she knew, too, had to be reached. There help would surely be waiting for her. Now whether the river really existed, she didn't have an idea. But she wasn't studying too much on that.

At the nearby plantation, her friends gave her a pair of brown shoes - soles rubbed with garlic. That was to keep the bloodhounds from tracing her. They also gave her a small bundle of food - some bread, fried fat-back, and cornpones. Then Granny, with Momma held tight, was driven in a wagon to a shallow stream. The famous river.

The wagon stopped. Granny jumped down. Momma woke

up, but didn't make a sound. Then the wagon tore away. Granny stood left completely alone with Momma in her arms. But she wasn't scared. She didn't have time for any such foolishness. She flung her shoes off, held her baby fast to her, and quick waded into the stream. It was fast moving water, and cutting cold. One time she slipped - near fell, but she kept on. Wasn't no turning back for her now. She stepped onto the other shore. Momma had never even moved an inch. Her big, round eyes had just stared up at Granny with love.

Darkness was fast shutting in through the thick-set trees. This was absolutely a new world to Granny…maybe chuck full of snakes, wild animals, or ghosts that could do dreadful things. Every tree, leaf, and shrub stood out double black and double scary. But Granny wasn't stopping to pay any of this any mind. No, sir. She pulled on her garlic-rubbed shoes, and set to poking for the path. She knew it had to be there somewhere. Sure enough…a almost not-to-be seen track went in through the trees. She ran right into that darkness and kept going miles on miles.

Now from what I heard Granny say, croton oil doesn't act as fast as castor oil. So she had at least two to three hours start before the dose actually begin working on the family. While it wouldn't kill any of them. They would hardly have time to think of her being gone, until she was miles away. But she wasn't trusting to that. So she flew along with Momma in her arms, still not making the tiniest sound.

Even though Momma was a good baby, Granny couldn't help getting weary. As time went on Momma got heavier and weightier, until Granny thought she couldn't move one more step, less her arms would break right off. Darkness was so tight around her now. She couldn't make out where she was heading anyway. She had only faith and God to guide her. Several times she had heard bloodhounds howling a way back. One time some big thing had rushed passed her. Thank God it decided to run on. She sighed with relief. Suddenly there was a loud cry like a screaming animal screams when in fear or anguish. Granny held her breathe. Then there were several loud hoots as something crashed off through the tree tops. Granny slowly released her breathe, and whispered to Momma, "Only an old owl, love…." But she knew she could not move one more step without dropping Momma. Possibly falling square on her. Besides, it was so friendly, so snug under those bushes....

Next thing, Granny heard voices. Men's voices. She felt her eyes open. She hadn't even realized they had been shut! It was daylight! Blinding bright daylight! The men's voices sounded nearer! They would sure find them! Momma started whimpering. Granny quickly stuffed her shawl into Momma's mouth. The men's voices were right on them! Holding her baby tightly...fear gripped Granny for the first time. She squeezed her eyes shut. She wanted to shut these men out! She prayed to God to make these men not real, if she didn't see them! A heavy boot kicked against her! A man yelled, "Someone's hiding!" She heard herself say, "Please, don't hurt my baby...." Then there was a moment of heavy silence - so thick and hot that Granny thought she would suffocate. The world seem to fall on her.

When Granny finally opened her eyes, she was surrounded with big men in shabby blue uniforms. This was a great and God-given relief - they were General Ulysses S. Grant's soldiers. Lord, they were on the colored leader's side... President Abraham Lincoln... thank goodness for Frederick Douglass. One soldier was tickling Momma, who was cooing and laughing again, like the happy baby she was. And Granny's mouth tasted like some licker had been poured down it.

"Where you from?" A heavy-set, older soldier asked Granny, as he blow smoke from his pipe.

Granny held Momma close to her. "Mississippi, sah"

"Where are you going?" She told him she had just aimed to get to the Union Side. She had been told they would help her. "We certainly will," the soldier said, "you're on the Union Side." Then Granny clutching Momma tightly to her breast was sat on a horse. Eventually, they landed in St. Louis where they have been ever since.

Chapter 3

It was between the ages of four or five that I developed a desire to have things my own way. I wanted to boss my playmates and my brother, Guy. Even though he was two years my senior, he was always calling, "Momma, make Tutti behave."

I was a very matter-of-fact kid, too. Even before starting kindergarten, I'd gather the other kids to tell them stories and fantasies. Sometimes I'd sing them songs I made up. These held them spellbound, and I was considered the wonder of the neighborhood.

St. Louis is the one town that always seems to have been a thriving town. It was and is mostly populated by Germans, who were very thrifty people. They were sure interested in good schooling, too. The St. Louis school system was said to be one of the best in the United States. Although we had no mixed-race schools with the exception that some of the Domestic Science and kindergarten teachers were white.

When I was six years old - along about 1890, I entered kindergarten at L'Ouverture School. The school was named after Toussaint L'Ouverture, the colored Haitian ruler. Owen Woods, who was real brainy and sought after by all woman, was principal. It was he who founded the first manual-training school in the city. Possibly in the entire country. Not even the white schools had the manual-training advantages we had.

I loved school and was always anxious to get there. I was very ambitious. So I was always ahead in games and classes, and the teachers' praises made me doubly eager to get farther.

My brother, an invalid, was naturally an extremely irregular attendant. So I'd hurry home to try to teach him what I'd learned. At times he listened, but other times he wouldn't. That provoked me, and I attempted to chastise him. Which didn't seem to work out so good. Momma usually whipped me in return. I always got even, however, when she wasn't home by whipping him.

Then one day out of a clear blue sky, Momma decided whipping me daily wasn't helping much. So she put me in a dark closet. Now fear was a thing I'd never known. So I sat calmly on the floor. After she thought I'd been in the dark long enough, she called me to eat. I completely ignored her. Asking Guy for the lamp to light the dark closet, I just sat there in awkward silence for fifteen or twenty minutes more. Finally after my stomach started growling, I answered her hauntingly, "I would rather stay where I am. I'm not hungry." Momma laughed heartily, and let me out. I gulped down my supper so fast, it would have made your head swim.

As the months went by, Momma began to feel the strain of too much hard work. She'd had a fair education, even though she had to learn along with the white people's children where Granny worked. So she resolved to try for a school teacher's position. She took an ordinary first grade grammar school examination - the kind like kids take in school now - passed, and was assigned to a small school in Farmington, Missouri.

Momma left us, and Granny took complete charge. I didn't miss her too much. Granny had always had as much to do with our raising as Momma. And thank God, Granny didn't beat me as much either. Yet, she still kept the same washboard and flat-iron noises filling our house.

When I finished second grade - Granny fell ill and Momma was called home. She looked happier than ever and was upside-down with excitement about her new life. She had joined a Methodist Church in Farmington, and met the presiding elder - a minister - who had charge of several churches in St. Louis and southeast Missouri. Momma became engaged to him. This wonderful minister was going to visit us, when he came to town. So she was immediately changed from the Trinity Baptist Church to St. Paul's Methodist Church. He was officiating there.

That all pleased me so much, I turned cartwheels and tumbled gleefully in the backyard. St. Paul's was the biggest, finest colored church in St. Louis. All my schoolmates and their parents went to it. It had room for fifteen hundred people, as well as this tremendous pipe-organ that made the most heavenly music. It lifted me up until I could scarce sit still. It made me see all kinds of pictures in my mind. It made me feel God was looking straight at me!

I went to church every chance I could. The music kept filling my head with all kinds of strange and different pictures. I felt I wanted to be there always. It made me so distant from everything I knew. Unfortunately after a few months home, Momma's funds gave out. She'd only made on the average of twelve dollars a month. That hadn't gone very far. We had always raised a few chickens for our own use. So it was decided to raise more for selling. It went so well, that we had four to five hundred chickens around Lent and Easter. We sold almost every one of them and their eggs.

We had done extra swell by Easter Sunday morning. So I brought all the white kids for blocks around to the house. Momma and Granny gave away dozens of coloured eggs. That made me a real neighborhood big-shot.

Then during the Chicago World Fair that high and mighty neighborhood position became even more set. A German delegation was passing through St. Louis, and visited L'Ouverture School. It was "the occasion" and we had been practicing weeks ahead to sing "Der Vacht um Rhine" in German. I'd never sung any German before. However, I was so chesty when the Germans singled me out to tell me how beautifully I sang, and with a perfect German accent!

Though most devilish, I was usually the monitor when the teacher left the room. That made me feel most stern. I was even strict with my pals. I felt even more important than usual, seated on the teacher's platform; feet not near touching the floor; spotless in a frilled white apron; hair twisted up with bright red ribbons, and at least six imitation gold bracelets of various sizes clanking on my arm. I truly felt high and mighty. I was acting like a female God searching out private wickedness.

One time Mamie Wilkins, a girl much older than me, got disorderly. She stuck some pins in the toe of her shoes. Then when no one was looking, she put her feet under the desk, and pricked the leg of the kid in front. That kid let out such a piercing howl that it made the hairs on our heads stand straight up! Mamie looked mighty pleased with herself. In spite of her being larger, and having a terrible reputation as a bully, I reported her at once. She was whipped with a rattan. It was her turn to howl now. The class enjoyed all this to no end.

Mamie hung her head for a moment before she walked up the aisle. She had one hand holding her backside, and the other wiping tears from her eyes. She turned and glared at me with a revengeful look. "I'll get you - teacher's pet! I'm gonna give you some walloping!"

I stared back at her, and snarled, "If you start up, you won't have the easy time you think."

School seemed to be over very quickly. We all came out together. Instead of Mamie going home, she followed me. In fact, most of the class trouped along. They didn't want to miss the action. When we were two blocks from school, we stopped at a vacant lot. As I started to put my books down, Mamie swung at me. I quickly ducked, my books falling to the ground. Thank goodness she missed. She swung at me so hard she knocked herself off balance. I trembled with a mixture of fear and anger, straightened up, and landed my fist smack in her mouth. Two teeth fell out. The rest of the time Mamie remained in school, she was one of my staunchest friends.

    School was so much pleasure, I hated to miss it. But with all the loving education, I just couldn't stop talking even during class. The teacher didn't know what to do. Finally, she made me sit with the boys. That was the supreme punishment. I was now definitely a "fallen kid." I went on being "fallen" until she found out, instead of being punishment, it was a delight. We'd hold hands, whisper love words…. "No lady ever behaves like that!" the teacher announced irritably, and changed her punishment. She kept me in after school - making me clean blackboards. That worked. I'd be late getting home, so Momma would whip me good, which did not appeal one bit. The whip was made of a leather strap.

    All this was in school and more. Always I was organizing - the "Dirty Dozen." This was a handkerchief-masked female aggregation for the pure, simple purposes of making teachers' lives miserable. I even organized St. Louis' first colored female basketball team. We tore around in blue bloomers, white sweaters, and brought lots of old people's wrath down on us. They said how shameful and unladylike it was to disport in such undress! We didn't pay them no mind. We forged on until at practice, I ran head on into a brick wall. That ended our basketball careers. All the elders said it was the hand of God.

    Ever since I had any kind of memory, I remember always singing, no matter what I was doing. Everybody around me sang whenever they could. They scarce gave it a thought. In the fifth grade, however, they taught us how to read music notes! That was probably the most important day of my childhood. It sent me into a complete new world. It made me realize to be able to sing, and to know what you were singing, were two entirely different things. I, also, loved looking over maps and pictures of places…wondering would I ever get to them. They all looked so wonderful. I decided I had to get to them some day. So music and geography became my favourite studies.

Chapter 4

With growing older, an ugly hatred sprung up between the whites and blacks. Instead of being pals, I was "Nigger!" Once in awhile someone said a casual, "Hello," but that was extremely rare. Mostly, I was completely alone. I couldn't understand that. Why shouldn't the whites who had been my friends, keep on being friends? I wanted to be their friend.

One Saturday I was shooting marbles with a group of white boys - who decided it was okay to let me play with them that one time. My brother, whose ambition was to become a minister, sat quietly reading his Bible in his usual place - a hollow where some of the pickets had been torn from our fence. So I wasn't playing too far from Guy, because he was liable to go into a fit anytime. Usually at the full moon.

Some grown-up white boys from another neighborhood, walked across the street towards the house. They began yelling, "Nigger! Nigger!" while they punched Guy in the face. Guy screamed painfully, pleading with them to stop, before he fell over writhing with pain. The white boys that I was playing with grabbed their marbles, quickly running down the street. They didn't care if several big boys were hurting an invalid colored boy. Besides he was a "Nigger" wasn't he? The grown-up white boys continued to beat on Guy. I wasn't just furious. I was purple with rage. Rage for not only beating on Guy, but rage at a society that hated us simply because of our colour. I angrily threw rocks at the boys…angrily throwing rocks at all the hatred for me and Guy…hatred that was not of my doing.

Finally one of the rocks smashed into a boy's head. He instantly dropped to the ground. I was satisfied then, and tore back to Guy. He was laying in the dirt - foam oozing from his lips, and the corners of his mouth. So as carefully as I could, I dragged him into the house, soothingly saying, "It's gonna be all right now…it's fine now."

Pretty soon the boy I'd hit and his people came to Momma with "Dutch Fritz," the policeman.

The sandy blonde boy pointed at me with an arrogant smugness, "That's the nigger knocked me down!"

Dutch had been on our beat for years. "Georgie is

mischievous (I wondered how he knew my name?) but not bad. You must have done something to her."

"He did," I said, and then took Dutch into where Guy was laying on the bed moaning with his bruised face.

Dutch marched right back to the white people. "If I catch that boy of yours in this neighborhood again, I'll lock him up!"

The boy's father's eyes narrowed as they blazed with pure hatred, then he sneered, "You should lock her up! Damned niggers! Don't know when they have it good! We'll run them out of town, if they don't keep their place!"

I thought about all that a lot. The boy who had beaten Guy was at least four to five years older. He'd hurt Guy badly, but nothing happened to him. Such things caused me to believe, that most whites were never gonna ever like me either. So without wanting it, in me was born the desire to fight. To protect my people, whenever, wherever the occasion demanded.

I began to hate the sound of washboards and flat-irons. They added up to how those whites had felt about us. I thought and studied on how I could make it. I wasn't gonna slave with Granny, Momma, and the other colored people, just to scratch out a living. The only way out, I knew, was studying real hard. I'd be so good, that I could become a school teacher. Also, vaguely, I heard of people making their living by singing. That, I made up my mind, was even better than being a school teacher. So out of hate, and humiliation were born the first seeds of my future.

We lived on the south side of St. Louis. But lots of other colored school kids lived on the north side. They were forced to go home through an Irish district called Kerry Patch. The Patch kids always waited to beat up the colored kids. So I'd run home soon as school was out. Throw on my war-jacket (Guy's sack coat) with one pocket full of marbles and the other rocks. Then I'd rush back, get with the kids from the north side, and fight my way through Kerry Patch. Usually, the whole bunch would get home safe. However, I'd have to get Dutch Fritz to see me back home. That was the first protecting my colour I ever did.

Chapter 5

When I was about ten years old, I sang at my first concert - a real school affair. All the kids performed, but I had a solo, "The Spider And The Fly." I wore my white dotted Swiss dress, a pair of my precious patent leather shoes, the bright red ribbons in my hair, all my imitation gold bracelets, and was ready and dressed hours before the great event.

When my turn came, I wasn't scared a bit. I just stood straight before everybody, stuck my chest out, opened my mouth, and sang my heart out. To me this particular singing was so much fun, because lots of people were hearing me - not only Momma, Granny, and Guy, but loads of friends.

After I finished my song, everyone clapped and yelled, "More! Sing some more!" Suddenly, I was real scared. I rushed off the platform. I wouldn't go back. I couldn't. I hid behind a desk.

Somebody said, "Georgie Harvey is scared!" Me...scared! I never heard such talk. I got up and smoothed my pretty dress. Then back on the platform I went and sang twice more - "A Little Brown Bird" both times. I'd have sung it some more, but teacher said twice was enough. Everybody else said what a wonderful voice I had. How I was going to be another Black Patti! After that evening, all I could think of for a long time was Black Patti. How Black Patti was named after white opera star Adelina Patti. How she was said to be the greatest colored singer, and had even sung in Europe.

That same year I heard Momma talking about how Black Patti's Troubadours were coming to St. Louis to sing. How a man by the name of Bob Cole, who created "A Trip To Coontown," had worked with Sissieretta Jones in conceiving Black Patti's Troubadours. How they had toured widely to great acclaim. Then huge posters were stuck up all over town. They were life sized pictures of Sissieretta Jones as Black Patti - very queenly in this long white dress, with a long white trail, and long white gloves all the way up her arms. Her hair was done pompadour style. She seemed a light brown skinned woman - sort of my colour. I looked and looked at her picture - up and down - how could I get to hear her sing? Then I noticed on the poster that Sissieretta said, "The flowers absorb the sunshine because it is their nature." I posed putting my hand over my heart, while pretending to be Black Patti, "I give out melody because God filled my soul with song."

When I asked Momma to take me, she said she didn't have either the time nor money. There was the usual washing and ironing to be done. I thought and wondered. I went downstairs. Johnny Divine, who lived downstairs, was sitting on the front steps.

He smiled proudly, "Pop's gonna take me to hear Sissieretta Jones - none other than Black Patti's Troubadours."

"Momma doesn't have time to take me. She's got too much washing." Johnny looked sympathetic. He made money selling papers. I sat right down next to him - cried and wept, "Momma would really love to take me," I pleaded, "but…she doesn't have any money…and I want to go so bad. Oh…."

"I got a quarter," he said, "you can have it." He fished it out of his pocket. I stopped wailing immediately, grabbed the quarter, and flew away like a shot. I had to make sure he didn't change his mind, or Momma didn't come out and catch me.

This was the first time I'd ever been in a theatre. But I was so set on seeing Black Patti, I didn't pay any mind neither to the right nor the left. I sat way up in what was called the "gallery." Although, even if I'd wanted to sit below, I couldn't. Colored people weren't allowed - they were only permitted in the "gallery." However, I didn't really care what section of the theatre I sat in. I was excited beyond belief just to be there. My heart, I was sure, was going to jump out from the fact I was going to see and hear Sissieretta Jones - Black Patti!

It got very dark, and the curtain went up. A man in a beautiful black shiny suit came forward. He said a lot of high-sounding words. At last, I heard, "Sissieretta Jones as Black Patti!" There she stood! - Exactly as her pictures - white gloves tight up her arms, pompadour, and all. She was not only elegant - Black Patti was dazzling.

She bowed and smiled, showing all her teeth. Everybody clapped. I did, too - only more energetic. It felt so good to be there. Boy, this time my heart was sure going to pop out of my mouth!

The orchestra blazed into a new coda, then slowly the movement became softer with the piano player being featured more. Black Patti stood most straight with her hands held together in front of her. She sang…it was like being wafted away. She sang "Comin' Through The Rye," and other things in strange languages I didn't understand.

When the curtain came down, there must have been a tremendous clapping, but I didn't hear it. I was too moved by the music to say a word. I just drifted out of the theatre automatically towards home. I knew only one thing. I was going to be a singer! I was going to sing in foreign countries! I was going to be exactly like Sissieretta Jones with a fine white dress trailing, long white gloves up my arms, a pompadour…. I stood on our doorstep. I faced the street. I smiled - showing all my teeth. That was the important part - to show all your teeth. I bowed far down as I could get. A hand yanked me up, and a well known voice announced, "Georgie, I'm gonna whip you to a inch of your life! I declare! Going in a dirty old red dress! Your hair not combed!"

"But Momma…." Didn't she have no respect for the future Black Patti?

Johnny Devine walked quietly upstairs. "Don't punish her, Mis' Harvey," he said in a kind and respectful voice. "You don't know how badly Georgette wanted to see Sissieretta Jones as Black Patti."

Momma just glared at me. Finally, after a long sigh, she said, "Go right in to bed."

I tore inside and straight to the looking-glass. I examined myself most carefully. If I lowered my lashes, showed my teeth, and shoved my bosom - such as it was - out, I noted with satisfaction a very slight, but definite resemblance to Black Patti!

Mrs. Henley, a white opera singer whose laundry Momma did, was the other great influence for my singing career. I carried Mrs. Henley's clothes back and forth. Usually she was practicing - sometimes the operatic things she was going to sing. I'd never heard any music like that. It was so wonderful. I would take as much time as I could standing at her back door, but never time enough. I always had other chores to do.

Mrs. Henley sang at Uhrig's Cave, a great outdoor garden where operettas and concerts were given. But I never had money to go there. Although, even if I had the money, my skin colour kept me out. So I'd just stand across the street, and listen very hard. I could almost hear all of the singing. Gosh, how I was so crazy about hearing absolutely every bit of it!

Sometimes Mrs. Henley gave teas for the local socialites

and intellectuals. Momma would prepare the cakes and little dainty things. She would let me come along to carry them into the parlour. Was I tickled to be around such great people. With my best dress and ribbons, I'd carry in the good things. I smiled brightly, while I looked at everybody in their fine clothes. After which, I'd run back into the kitchen singing with joy!

One time after I served the cakes, Mrs. Henley came into the kitchen. "Lucy, is that you singing?"

"No, Mis' Henley...it's Tutti."

"Well, for a little girl, she has an amazingly strong voice," she said with a genuinely friendly smile. "Tutti also has a wonderful personality...and as you know, Lucy, a personality...alive and moving along with strong training in singing is the key to a bright future."

Momma tenderly looked at me, then just laughed, as she tried to keep her hurt from showing. She had no money to even start to think of such a thing. Besides, she wanted me to be a school teacher of music. So we just went right on washing and ironing Mrs. Henley's clothes...waiting on the local socialites and intellectuals. Mostly, I was happy. But whether I was or not, I continued singing all the time - standing extremely straight, holding my hands together in front of me, showing all my teeth, and bowing and bowing.

Chapter 6

My family was most religious. So religion was a very sacred thing to me. I was always taught there was a Supreme Being without whose help we could do nothing. I believed that. Actually, anything Granny or Momma said to me was the Bible itself. Besides my own mind taught me - when I looked around and saw rocks, trees, the river - they weren't just there. They had to have a beginning…somewhere. I still believe this.

From the time I was a little bit of a kid, I was taken to church. I was taught to get on my knees every night, before going to bed, and faithfully say my prayers. Even though my prayers were usually said in a rush, "Please, dear God, free Momma and Granny from the hardships of the washtub and the ironing board, and I'll be a good girl." After hearing Black Patti, I added myself, "and I'll be extra good if you make me like Black Patti. Amen."

Sunday School was a most fascinating place, where they told wonderful strange stories. Most of which were unbelievable, but you knew they were true. Because the Bible, which was the word of God, said them. Anyway, kids got Sunday School cards for remembering the stories. The cards were especially precious. They were the only reading I had outside of my school books, and Bible.

Wrapping the cards up - first in a napkin, then in a newspaper, I put them carefully away in a drawer for safekeeping. Every time I put one away, I'd take all the others out. Then I'd place them along my own little desk, read them over, and put them all away again. I had quite a collection.

Loving religion and Sunday School cards, however, didn't keep me out of mischief. Me and Alice Johnson, my special colored pal, learned a popular made-up song to one of the hymns. One night while the congregation was singing the real words, we sang:

> "At the bar, at the bar,
> Where I smoked my first cigar,
> And the money in my pocket rolled away,
> It was there by chance
> I tore my Sunday pants
> And now I have to wear them every day!"

It created such a sensation that one of Momma's friends yanked us out of church, and took us home. There was the usual thrashing.

When revival time came around, right after New Year's, I was most happy. Although, I treasured New Year's Eve the most, because it was "Watch Night," everybody - good, bad, grown-up, small babies carried by their mothers and fathers - made it their business to get to the service at eight o'clock.

The people came trouping in wearing just what they had. Some with plain coloured head rags tied over their heads; some in gingham aprons; some very grand in bustles they'd treasured for years; others in gay red and blue bandanas, but all were spotlessly cleaned. The gingham aprons were so stiff with starch, they stood right out. The cloth dresses stood out, too, because sometimes as many as nine stiffly starched ruffled petticoats were under them.

Everybody had to be in church by five minutes to twelve. At that time, we all got on our knees for silent prayer. This would invoke blessings from God for the coming year. At midnight, bells, horns, whistles, all sorts of rejoicing noises broke out in the whole city. Then everyone rose up, shaking hands singing:

> "What a happy New Year!
> What a happy, what a happy, what a happy
> New Year!"

The older folks sang:
> "Before this time, nother year,
> I may be gone in some lonesome graveyard.
> Oh Lord, how long?"

Then tears would stream down their well-scrubbed faces. Shouting, rejoicing, and much praising the Lord was heard...this was the beginning of the revival season.

Especially for this season, an out-of-town evangelist was brought in - always a man. Them folks didn't believe in women preachers. The evangelist was always a most fiery speaker. He led the meetings for six weeks every night and afternoon.

Singers from different places were often brought in, too. One man was especially brought in each year. His voice was so powerful, you could hear it outside the church, even when everybody else was singing. He'd sing the same phrases over and over again, until almost everybody would get religion, and receive the Holy Ghost right away.

The "Moaner's Bench" was a chief feature of revivals. That was where wicked people - and everyone was wicked to begin with, even small babies - were called to try to seek religion, to do away with their sins. The old people gathered around this "Moaner's Bench," and from one to the other sang and prayed over the kneeling sinners. The spirituals rose people from their seats. They continued until someone felt their sins were forgiven, jumped up, and shouted, "Brothers and sisters, thank God, I'm free at last! All my life, I've been walking in darkness. Through prayer and wrestling with the devil, I've shaken off the chains of sin! I'm a new person...hallelujah, praise God. I intend, by the help of God, because it's only through his help...praise God, to lead a new life and walk in the straight and narrow path. Pray for me!"

Then the elders clap their hands, and stamp their feet in rhythm. They sing, the redeemed sinner sings, everybody sings. Then everyone rushes around clapping hands, shaking hands, singing, shouting to God, "Nother soul is saved, Lord! Nother soul is saved, Lord!"

Men tore off their coats, running around frothing at the mouth. They would shout, scream, get so carried away, that some of them would fall out rigid as if they were dead. Yet, no matter what forgetfulness their religious emotions went to - even when women's clothes flew over their heads - nothing sensual happened. It was all noise, excitement, wildness, while praising God. People couldn't resist the strong pull of the spirit.

The praying, singing, shouting, clapping hands, and stamping feet went on until daybreak. Then everyone went home, and to work. Although, all those who could, attended four o'clock prayer meeting. This was where sinners who hadn't got religion during the night meeting, continued to pray until they did.

All sorts of things happened at revivals. One old lady, Aunt Jenny, owed another, Sarah, for a stove. Aunt Jenny wouldn't pay Sarah. So one revival night, Sarah shouted, stamped her feet, prayed, and picked up a chair. She was so carried away by religion that she went straight to where Aunt Jenny was praying. Then she lifted the chair over Aunt Jenny's head, getting ready to bring it down, when one of the brothers butted in, "Have Aunt Jenny arrested, Sarah," he said kindly, "after all, this is the house of the Lord."

Sarah's eyes flashed, then clouded over, "No, honey, I not gonna do nothing. Praise God...I'll just let the Lord pay her off." Sarah sat the chair down, and went back to her singing and feet stamping.

"De Lord's a mighty good man, but he's powerful long in paying off his debts sometime." Aunt Jenny snapped back at Sarah, wiped perspiration from her forehead, then she went back to shouting and singing.

Since everybody was born in sin, Alice and me weren't any different. So when we were about twelve years old, we listened intently to the preacher's sermon. When he called for sinners, who wanted to be saved, we went up to the alter, and knelt down. The elders formed a circle around us praying, singing, and moaning for the Holy Ghost to come into us.

I truly felt sorry for the wicked things I'd done. I was always fighting, and talking in school. That was very wicked. Plus it upset Momma so. I thought on that, and felt most lowly. I prayed silently - Dear Lord, please forgive me. Dear Lord, I'll be a good girl, and never fight no more. The singing and stamping got louder, and faster... louder, and so fast, I began to feel light... extremely light. I swayed in time with the singing. I felt happy like a weight had been lifted from me. I rose up, swaying, yelling loud above the singing, stamping, and clapping. "Praise God... I'm... in his most holy name... Brothers and sisters, I gonna stick to my religion like it was a piece of meat and bread."

Everybody shouted even more, rejoiced, shook my hand, and one another's hands. I rushed home to tell Momma. She had been too busy washing and ironing to come that night. But she was sure happy to hear I'd got religion, and was a reformed child.

Every year in August, the colored churches of St. Louis had barbecue picnics on the town's outskirts. The churches chartered two or three big moving vans, fixed up plank seats in them, and dressed in our very best, we all piled in. With tons of laughs and giggles, off we went to the picnic grounds. Sometimes our picnic would be so grand that several horse-cars were chartered. However, this was only on the most grand occasions.

The men would get to the grounds about five in the morning. Then they would dig maybe six pits, six feet deep, build fires in them, and stretch halved sheep, hogs, and cows on poles over the flames. The fires were always made of hickory logs, whose smoke got into the roasting meat. This gave the meat that special smoked wood flavour that I loved. It was really good. We could smell it for blocks, before we came close to the picnic grounds. There were, also, lots of cakes, ice cream, soda water, and all sorts of thing to eat. But the barbecued meat was the main thing.

There was dancing with music y a hired band. They played "Shortnin Bread," "Annie Rooney," and "After the Ball," but I didn't care much for dancing that day. Everybody laughed a lot in a polite way. They were careful to show off their grand new clothes. They were puffed and flounced and embroidered and bejeweled with imitation jewels. Most of the time, I would have found this fascinating. Yet, today I wanted to do something different, besides just looking at each other, and acting sedate. I was almost tired of the whole thing, especially the phonies, when someone said, "There's a Gypsy camp round here!" Now that sounded like something.

"I'm gonna hunt for those Gypsies!" I was thrilled at the thought of it.

"Don go near 'em! They'll steal yuh, sure!" One of the other kids warned me.

I smiled at him, and quickly sauntered towards the Gypsy camp. I was very pleased that nobody came with me. I wanted to find out for myself whether Gypsies really had ponies? Whether they really lived in vans and could tell fortunes? I especially wanted to hear my fortune.

Suddenly a beautiful young girl with mysterious, melting, dark eyes stood face to face with me. She was carrying a baby. It was incredible how they seem to appear out of the air!

"Want your fortune told?" the Gypsy asked in a calm quiet manner.

"I have no money...."

"You have plenty."

How did she know I had thirty-five cents? Twenty-five for my barbecue, and ten for my carfare. I had thought about eating that barbecue for weeks. I tried to make up my mind.

"You are going to travel much...."

I forgot the barbecue, and dropped the quarter into her hand, which was filthy. In fact, she and the baby were absolutely the filthiest people I'd ever seen.

"You feel things... everything. That's written on your face. You will marry. It will not last. You will go to a big city.

From there, you will take a ship. You will travel for years by land and sea. There is a fine life to be lived. Through disaster, at the height of this fine life, you will lose everything…almost your life! The rest is all dark.…"

"Will I ever get back what I lose?" I asked in a rush.

"Maybe.…" She ran away. I stood stock still - fascinated - wondering about "maybe." I still wonder about that "maybe.…"

Chapter 7

Colored people, particularly older ones, have a lot of superstitions. A picture falling from the wall is a sign of that person's death. A cold wind felt while walking by a empty house is a spirit passing by.

A girl friend of mine had been born with a caul over her face. She said it allowed her to see spirits. There were times when we would just be walking along and she would suddenly say, "Move over, Georgie! Let that man pass!" I didn't ever see anyone - man or woman, but I would move over as quickly as I could.

At this girl's house, one time when she was making up the bed, she raised a sheet...stood stock still, eyes straight out, "Oh, look at that spirit! It raised right up with the sheet. Somebody's gonna die!" Three days later, her brother-in-law... cleaning windows...lost his balance and fell down. He was killed instantly.

Another time when she came to our house, and we were sitting in the front room just talking, she said out of a clear blue sky, "A child died in this room!"

"Whatever makes you say that?" I asked with dead seriousness.

"Well, look at that beautiful little girl playing. She's so happy. Look at her running around!" I looked but I didn't see a thing. A few weeks later some Irish people, living across the street, told me a little girl had died in that very room!

I couldn't see the spirits, because the caul I'd been born with had been lost. But I'm forced to believe in all this, since I've seen so many things that my girl friend said come true. Granny, too, said seamen would pay any price for a caul. No disaster had ever happen if they had one on board a ship.

One night in May 1896, when I was twelve years old, Guy and me went to sleep as usual in our trundle bed. That was at nine o'clock, and we fell soundly asleep. Along about midnight, I found myself sitting straight up in bed! Seemed to be three sharp knocks! - from the front door, but the front door was wide open! I pushed Guy, but he didn't even open his eyes - just grunted.

"Guy, wake up!"

"Aw...what d'yuh want?" He still kept his eyes shut.

"Did you hear that knocking."

"Naw… ain't nobody knockin… go on sleep…"

He turned over - asleep again. I listened very hard, but everything was most still. Maybe, I'd been mistaken. Probably dreamed it. I laid back down. Three knocks again - louder, sharper, on the kitchen door! That wasn't dreaming! I'd heard them distinctly!

"Momma! Granny! Did you hear that knocking?" They had heard it, simultaneously with me! Instantly, they were out of bed. I jumped up, too. We all rushed out on the porch. Maybe someone was there? No - nobody. There was a moment of silence, then Granny shook her head wondering-like, but she didn't say a thing. She only looked dreadfully solemn. We all slowly walked back into the bedroom.

We went to our beds, and raised the covers to get in - three knocks again - on the downstairs front door! This time the knocks were so loud, we thought they would tear everything down! We all heard them - Guy even sat up in bed. Even the downstairs people rushed out shouting, "Lucy! Did you hear that?"

Granny looked more dreadful solemn than before. "Somebody's going," she said, her voice suddenly sounded tired, strained…almost resigned, and we believed it was the truth. Momma turned the lamp up bright. When it was almost morning, and we couldn't sit no more, we went to bed.

One week later to the very day, May 27, 1896, I got up around five o'clock, as usual, to let the chickens out. It was hot as Billy-be-damned! That was most unusual. In May, that time of the morning, it was never very hot. The chickens fed, I went back into the house. Everybody else was up. We all quietly ate our oatmeal, biscuits, molasses, and milk.

Our Cousin Wallace, who was seventeen years old, was living with us. This was only since his mother, my aunt, had died. We were pleased to have him. He did chores around town, and gave Momma all the money he made, which helped a lot. That morning he could hardly eat anything. It was that hot!

"Sure is hot…." I told one of the kids on the way to school, while we slowly walked in the baking sun.

Florence, a fat avocado-shaped girl, sighed as she wiped the sweat from her forehead with a small pudgy hand. "My Mammy says it ain't never been so hot before. It's wickedly hot."

The heat grew more and more intense as the day went on.

It was such a scorcher that our clothes were so wet with sweat, they were sticking miserably to our skin. We could barely sit in our seats.

At twelve everybody meandered home for lunch. When I got home the house was completely quiet. Granny and Momma weren't washing or ironing or anything - just sitting slouched down, exhausted by the heat. It was almost impossible to get your breath. Everything was so humid that I found myself wishing for the snow. At least in the winter, I could put on a lot of clothes, and sit by the stove making myself comfortable...but with this wretched heat, there was no relief anywhere.

After lunch somehow I drifted back to school. But at two-thirty it became unbearably hot, so school was dismissed. Everybody went home excepting Jimmy White, Sis Henderson, and myself. We stayed to help arrange the program for the graduating kids.

We had only gone over two or three songs when the room seemed to grow hauntingly dark. Then it began to thunder... the room grew even darker. Jimmy White nervously walked over to the window and looked out. "Hey! Commerce! Look!" A mass of black clouds in wave-like formation covered the whole sky! A wind took to moaning. That made it even more awesome. It moaned louder, and higher. The classroom was nearly dark now. "Let's get out of here. Something's gonna happen!"

"Maybe, a hail storm," I placed the sheet music back inside the closet, "but whatever it is... it's kinda eery."

Sis frowned, a bit of panic in her voice. "Yeah, they happen like that in hot weather... not always good my Momma use to tell my Auntie."

"See you tomorrow!" I tore down the street. Everybody almost everywhere I looked was getting under shelter. You couldn't hardly see a cat out. Wind seemed to be all around me, buzzing like a ever-whizzing saw. The thunder got louder. By now it was almost completely dark. Yet, still it seemed to keep getting darker and darker all the time. Lightening flashed...I stumbled along blindly for a few seconds. I rushed through our gate like Satan was behind me.

I could barely see Momma frantically flying around, gathering clothes in from the line in the yard...Granny rushing upstairs with arms full of clothes, while the two downstairs kids were madly chasing the chickens, trying to get them into their sheds. Through the roar of the wind, I heard Momma shouting, "Tutti, hurry up! Help chase the chickens in!" Then she grabbed the last of the clothes, and dashed upstairs.

I ran to help gather the chickens. By this time the fierce wind was roaring so strong, I could hardly stand up! The dust was really stinging my eyes now. I was nearly blind. It got darker - still darker! Window glasses crashed. A terrific thunder boomed. Lightening tore everything open - shut it all up again. I grabbed the kids, stumbling towards the house. Somewhere… in a distance-like… Momma yelled something. "Stay downstairs with the kids! Wallace'll come down with you!" The wind tossed us around as if we were straw dolls. Yet, I clung tightly to the children…desperately holding them with every ounce of strength I had. Finally, what seemed like forever, Wallace lumbered down to us. He groped around for my hand, but the darkness was so thick, I could almost touch it. He reached out again… the wind howled louder… finally Wallace grabbed one of my hands, but the wind ripped us apart again.

Finally, all of us got inside the door. A big ball of red lightening hit against the iron street light. It was amazing! The pole that was always in front of our house snapped in two! Nothing but roaring thunder, wind lashing at us from every direction, glass crashing into slivers everywhere. I turned towards the kitchen. But the kitchen wall came towards me! I pulled at the door. I wanted to get out! A great, cracking, ripping, tearing…" Momma! Momma…!"

…Some sort of noise…such aching, throbbing, beating…. Some sort of regular sound…consistent noise… such pain…chop, chop…chopping. Voices. Men's voices!…so far away. I shut my eyes, which made me realize they had been open. I couldn't tell otherwise, because it was so black. I opened them again. It seemed to be lighter. I seemed to be laying on the ground, flat on my face. A face was right next to mine… it was wet and muddy and…unshaven…Wallace! The chopping came quite clear now, and a voice distinctly cried, "Where is my child? Where is my child?" Sounded like Momma.

Several men's voices, "She must be along here." The chopping was almost in my ear. Suddenly, everything grew crystal clear! "I'm all right, Momma! Don't let them chop anymore! In here…they're chopping over my head!" The chopping stopped. Only the sound of Momma crying over and over, "Thank God for saving my child!"

Then I heard the wooden screeching noise made by prying up boards. I tried to help them get to me faster by shouting, "A little bit to the left! Here! Over here!" Suddenly, a miracle...a small brighter space - a hole!...with light in it, dim yellow lights...lanterns. I smelt the rain! I felt the rain! Hands reached down, yanked me - I screamed with pain...everything got black again.

When I opened my eyes again to the light, I discovered the roof and ceiling (what had been our house) was resting on my left leg. The only thing keeping the full weight from me was our marble-topped mahogany table! More prizing, ripping boards, banging...my leg was free! But the pain! Such blinding, bleeding, all over pain! Finally, they dragged me out.

Air and rain poured over me...running all over my face and hands...so good and cold and alive! There's no way I could ever describe what it's like to be under an old house with earth, and rot in your nostrils and mouth; blackness in your eyes; and then the joy and blessing of the rain...the wonderful, sweet smelling rain!

I tried to stand up and grab ahold of Momma, but I fell. Quickly, she caught me, gently lowered me on a stretcher - such a burning in my leg! I gently touched Momma's face...she held my hand and kissed the palm, then she hugged me like she was never going to let me go.

"Where's Wallace?" Momma asked softly as she caressed my head.

"He's right back where I was...he's alright, isn't he?" I clung to Momma tightly, and she rocked, and she moaned, "Oh, Lord have mercy," while the men pulled more boards away. They found Wallace - dead. Right in the same place where we'd heard the last three knocks!

Momma's moaning grew louder, then she burst into tears as the men picked up my stretcher. "We'll carry her to the doctor's office. You stay with your son, Mrs. Harvey."

They carried me down the street. I hurt so, I couldn't even open my eyes. I was almost unconscious from the excruciating pain. Suddenly, there were great thunderclaps! Forkered lightening! More wind! Hail...rain...screaming, and wailing! "Nother cyclone! Nother cyclone!" Instantly the men dropped the stretcher, and raced off down the street. I lay there alone with rain beating against my battered body...people running right by me, but nobody stopping. It was almost impossible to get my body upright. But I dragged myself up, sort of ploughed down the street, through twisted wires, broken bricks, and glass.

A street car was overturned in front of the doctor's house...people lying all around it. I dragged myself passed it. A dirt cart was turned upside down - the horse still attached - it was dead. I pulled myself over the horse. I didn't care whether I was crawling across dead horses, or anything just so I got inside that house. My pain was so piercing...someone...some doctor there... that could stop the pain. I finally crawled in, and fell on the floor. There wasn't a single soul in the whole house...I laid there soaking wet, and almost out of my mind with hurting. Was God punishing me for something?

The violent forceful wind, and rain continued loud for a time. At last it died down, died down, and died... silence.... Then usual noises...like something scratching against the walls of the house. People moving outside...people talking...doctor, and some men came. The doctor looked at me. "Well, she's alive at least. Carry her to Hager's. Her people are there. I haven't time to treat her now - too many dead and dying!"

The next morning my leg ached terrible still. I was stiff all over, and it was freezing cold. Momma and me had to get going to the morgue, despite the grief, to identify Wallace. With the exception of him, we were all saved. Granny was out early, regardless of the icy weather, looking up some of her white people. She was trying to get money, and help for a new house.

Momma got me up, and helped me dress. Then she told me the marble-topped mahogany table had kept the roof off of them, too. They had crawled out - the only injury Momma had was when a looking-glass broke, cutting her above her eye.

The Hagar's (white people who lived next door to us) house hadn't even been touched. They had taken us in, and fed us breakfast. Mr. Hager even brought me some crutches, and Momma and me got going.

The first thing we noticed, as we walked across the small sodden grass strip in front of the Hagar's house, was the roof of the big oil mill. The oil mill had been a large place, employing fifty men - it had been blown a block away. Now its roof was sitting in our back yard. There wasn't a trace of our chicken sheds nor a sign of our five hundred chickens - just a few boards that had been our house, and a few sticks - hardly bigger than your hand - that had been our furniture, and one thing more...the marble-topped mahogany table! It was in perfect condition. But where the big old tree had stood in front of our house, was now a hole in the ground.

    West Jefferson Avenue was filled with bits of brick, pieces of furniture, and broken glass. "Did you hear about Old Granny Welsh?" a stunned and saddened neighbor stopped us. We shook our heads "no" very slowly. "Well, she sent little Aggie to get a loaf of bread, just before the storm. When the storm broke, Aggie was walking back. She got hit with a flying brick and knocked dead. After the storm Granny Welsh was sitting in her rocking chair, knitting needles in her hands, and a lap full of bricks. She was dead!" We had to pass by what was left of Granny Welsh's house - one brick wall.

    With my arms aching painfully from the crutches, me and Momma turned onto Chouteau Avenue. We stopped for a few sad moments, as we watched them taking out bodies in long baskets from the oil mill, where ten men had been killed. Further down on Chouteau and Maple Street, we passed by a house that had been lifted up, and turned completely around on its foundation. Yet, it stood intact. The furniture in it hadn't even been harmed!

    Another neighborhood German woman stopped us before we crossed the street to the morgue, "A woman stood in her doorway with her baby in her arms. The wind tore the infant from her." The old woman trembled, and held tightly to her cane as she sighed heavily. "The baby was later found dead, hanging by its little dress on a church steeple, six blocks from where the woman had stood!"

    Finally, after all of the heartbreaking stories, we reached the front of the morgue. It was a good sized white-stone building, that had a foreboding aura reeking from it. Momma held my crutches under one arm, I leaned on her other arm, hobbled up two steps, then we slowly went into a room full of tormented wailing and weeping - people packed so tightly - searching for kin and friends...agony was everywhere. We were told that no one had time to help us. That there were so many bodies, we'd simply just have to look around.

    Dead people were stacked up five or six on top of each other. It was just plain horrible. Thoughts of Mr. Rose's Dairy, Pork, and Slaughter House popped into my head, because of the inhuman way the bodies were lying on stretchers, or planks, or just hastily thrown together. Although, someone did have the decency to cover them with some black cloth like tarpaulin. After about fifteen minutes of peering at dead faces, my leg began to pain me so much, that I couldn't see…my head seemed to be burning, and the smell of death, made my breakfast rise from my stomach to my throat. I leaned against the wall, trying not to collapse onto the floor. Finally, some people helped me to a seat, while I fought the urge to vomit. But poor weary Momma continued to search.

It seemed like five hours later, when she sighed heavily, and dropped into the chair next to me. She had found Wallace. His neck had been broken. Out of seven hundred people killed, Wallace was the only colored one. We buried him from the undertaker's. We had no home to take him to for cooling, and a funeral.

Day and night something in my head banged. I couldn't sleep nor eat nor nothing. Even when someone talked to me, I could barely hear them. My head ached so intensely. I was only acutely aware of the pain. One day I felt like I would go completely crazy. Finally, Momma took me to the clinic. They found my scalp was full of glass and lime. Immediately, they cut my hair as short as possible, without hurting my head anymore. Then they extracted the junk. I didn't mind the pain at all, as long as they got rid of it forever.

What I did mind was the pained looks in Granny's and Momma's faces. Without chickens, they were again faced with the agony of just hard washtub and ironing-board labour.

Chapter 8

As soon as I felt well again, I heard the same, dreary, forever-sounding washboard rubbing, and flat-iron clanking. These weary noises went on way into four o'clock in the morning. I'd lay there almost every night, desperately trying to choke off the reality of the drudgery. I felt wretched that Momma and Granny had to slave like that. I worshipped them. Yet, I couldn't think of any way to stop their hard labours. I prayed night and day unceasingly, "Please, God, let me do something to help Granny and Momma!" I learned to iron shirts.

This was all too much worry and torture for Granny's aged shoulders. She got to ailing again, and had a breakdown. Momma found it impossible to carry on by herself. My ironing shirts wasn't much help. So Guy slipped off, and got a job driving a cart. That didn't last long. He had a fit, fell off the cart, and they carried him home half-conscious. We couldn't ever let him work again. There was just so much misery in our fine new home. We couldn't see how to go on much longer.

Roy Franklin, the minister Momma was suppose to be engaged to, paid us a visit. After a tasty meal of ham hocks, black-eyed peas, boiled chicken feet, and candied yams, we all sat around sipping lemonade. After Momma refilled our glasses, Reverend Franklin took his hand and placed it against her cheek. "I have an announcement to make. Since most of my affairs are now in St. Louis, I can board with you, and pay three dollars a week." Three dollars a week was our weekly rent! "Well..." Reverend Franklin smiled, looking at one of us to the other.

Finally, Granny said, "that's mighty charitable of you, Reverend...God bless you...a lot of Christian help right now."

Things looked much brighter now. We all not only liked Minister Franklin, but adored him. He was so charitable - always bringing us candy and fruit. Everybody we knew thought most highly of him.

Roy Franklin was a man around fifty-four years old. He was medium height, had smooth dark brown skin, mixed gray hair, and was fine looking. He dressed extremely well - suits and shoes always made to order. He was always so impressive with his little goatee and mustache. He was forever brushing both of them.

And, boy, was he sought after by the women! I was only thirteen, but I idolized him. He seemed to like me, too.

Having his head scratched with a comb was his favourite pastime. He'd say, "Tutti, I'll give you a dime if you scratch my head." I'd run get his blue comb, and stand between his knees. Then I'd scratch his head. He'd hold me close, pet me, kiss me - sometimes on the mouth! It was all so wonderful. I'd throw my arms around his neck, and kiss him back. After fifteen or twenty minutes, he'd suddenly push me away, give me a dime - sometimes a quarter! - saying, "Run along now and play. I'm going to take a nap."

Momma was crazy about watermelon, cantaloupes, and sardines with crackers. I'd take the money Minister had given me, and buy her those things. Sometimes for a special surprise, I'd get her a handkerchief. She was always so pleased. It was better all around having Minister live with us. We had survived tremendous poverty that would have normally destroyed other families. Now Momma didn't have to work so hard, and we had all sorts of little comforts for Granny. What I was truly pleased about was that Guy had someone to talk Bible and God with...he finally had a friend, who enjoyed talking about the prophets in the Old Testament like Samuel, Isaiah, and Jeremiah.

That summer and fall, it rained all the time. An epidemic of measles, also, broke out. Guy caught them, and Granny put him immediately in bed. She didn't call the doctor. But made sage tea, which everyone knew was a sure-fine-long-tried remedy for any ailing problem. Invariably working better than any doctor's medicine.

For three weeks, Guy was in bed. Then he got well. He went out to deliver some washing for Momma, got caught in the rain on the way back...he was soaking wet, and shivering when he walked through the door, and instantly had a relapse. Only this time, he went into galloping consumption.

Momma was sending me to the drug store - exactly three weeks later, when Guy weakly said, "Momma, it's so dark. Why don't you light the lamp?" It was very light, but she said nothing. She knew he was probably blind. Guy continued, "Take care of Skippy for me. Don't let the dog catcher get him." Momma and Granny pressed their hands against their mouths. I went on to the store. When I got back, crying was in our house. Guy was laying with his arms folded cross-wise on his chest. He was dead.

I cried a lot, but I knew deep within my heart that Guy was better off. He had suffered so much pain from being afflicted with epilepsy. Not being able to work like other boys, really disturbed him, too. He had surely gone to a better life. I knew when a person died, they just passed from this life to another - the good people to a better life. The wicked to a worse one. Perhaps, Guy was up in the clouds with the angels... preparing to walk through the Heavenly Gates of Pearls.

Granny and Momma missed Guy something awful. They would spend evenings, near the warmth of the stove, talking about what a good boy he was, and how empty they felt without him. However, Minister agreed with me, he felt Guy was better off. That by the Lord taking him, it was one more burden lifted off the backs of Granny and Momma. They didn't see it that way. Momma and Granny continued to wear their mourning clothes.

Chapter 9

Feeling mentally and physically stronger one year later, Granny thought she could do a little work. People living in the suburbs called her to deliver a white child. So she went.

Around nine o'clock at night, about a week later, we heard yelling outside. Momma put the book done she was reading, and leaned forward in her chair. "Who can that be?" Momma stated puzzled. "Tutti, you stay here. Someone wants me on the telephone over at the grocery."

"Well, must be big news, Momma." We hardly ever got telephone calls. Momma wasn't listening to me, she just wrapped a shawl tightly around her shoulders, and ran out. I pressed my nose to the window. I wasn't gonna miss nothing. It started to rain slightly... raindrops thinly spotted the glass. Then all of a sudden, I felt a distinct chill...something was wrong. Soon Momma came rushing upstairs. She was panting loudly, and panicky. "They're going to bring Granny home! She's sick!"

My insides twisted together so tightly, I had to grasp for breathe myself, "What's the matter with her?"

"I don't know! They didn't say! Oh, God be merciful!" We changed the linen on the bed, and fluff up the pillows. We put the kettle on to heat some water. Then we ran around making things to do. We were too nervous to just sit still. Momma kept calling on God to be merciful. Finally, what seem like forever, we heard a horse and wagon, galloping down the street. It stopped in front of our door. Momma ran downstairs with me right behind her. I didn't know how truly frightened I really was, but my insides were screaming - Granny was my everything... my hopes, my dreams, my life...our strength.

Then some strange men carried Granny in, "She's paralyzed on her right side," one of them mumbled. Granny forced a smile and whispered, "Don't worry, Lucy. I'll be all right." The strange men placed her in bed. Then they tramped away, leaving a heavy smell of tobacco. Me and Momma sit next to the bed... a hollow sadness came into us.

The next morning, Granny seem to feel better. She asked for her quilt pieces. She loved to make crazy, bright coloured quilts. When I brought her the pieces, Granny tried to pick them up. She couldn't. Her right hand was totally paralyzed. Granny laid the bright bits down with her left hand. "Never min...."

Watching Granny this way, filled my whole body with crying. I fought hard to keep my tears from spilling over, and stiffly walked out on the porch. I sat in a huddle with my dress pulled down over my knees. There was a cold wind off the Mississippi River that gave me a chill.

Momma fixed Granny some vegetable soup, left it next to the bed, and went back into the kitchen. When she came back, Granny was laying with her eyes shut. "She's sleeping... that's good." Then Momma moved to the chest-of-drawers to get some fresh pillowslips. Suddenly, she turned away from the chest, and hurried to the bed. She bent over Granny. She touched her. She screamed...kept on screaming, and screaming, and screaming! Momma's whole body was shaking like a leaf, when I grabbed her. With my face against her shoulder, I wrapped my arms tightly around her, as we seemed to drown in a sea of tears. Some neighbors rushed in, and gently pulled us apart. They led Momma into the living room, to her favourite chair. She was so full of grief. It was as if Momma didn't know anything or anyone, but misery.

When Granny died it was like a part of us was taken. She was wise, good, and always shielded me. After many days and nights of crying, I finally got over her death. Momma never did. Finally, Mrs. Turner, who lived next door, told Momma, "Granny informed me a few weeks ago, 'Miz Turner, I have a presentiment I won't be here long. Don you tell Lucy, but if anything happens help her much as you can.'" All Momma did was fold her arms tightly in front of her, and sob. I'd never known so many sobs were in the world.

Mrs. Turner, with the help of some of the other neighbors, washed Granny, while she lay in bed. Then they laid her on the cooling board. Which was nothing but two ironing boards put together, that were stretched on four chairs. The very same ironing boards that Granny had laboured over so tirelessly, ever since she had freed herself, and settled in St. Louis.

After Granny was laid out in the front room, Mrs. Turner made a great big pot of coffee. Then people brought in food - ham, boiled eggs, and bread. That night all of Granny's friends began to arrive all clean, as if they were going to revival meeting.

They came in and walked straight up to the coffin one by

one. Then they would stand there for several moments, just affectionately looking at Granny in her gray cashmere shroud. Finally, they all sat down around the coffin, looking very serious in the dim coal-oil, rose-smelling lamp light. Some sobbed quietly, and others said gently, "Poor Mary, she's at rest, and her work is done. Yea, the African warrior flowed down the Mississippi River back to Mother Africa." I could hear Momma crying, and carrying on in the bedroom. It was all so terrifying to me...the smell of all the beautiful flowers was so heavy and sweet, they made me sick.

Granny's friends tenderly sang old religious songs. Their voices were all the sad things, I'd ever felt in my life. And some I'd never known before.

After this they went out into the kitchen, and solemnly ate the food. Some finished eating and went home, but others kept on arriving. This went on until the next day, when Granny was carried away.

On Christmas Day they lowered the pinewood coffin, through the sparkling white snow, into the hard cold earth. They said, "Ashes to ashes...Dust to dust," and Momma fainted. The church bells toiled exact, and dreadful. Granny's friends, since slavery days, started singing slowly, and tenderly again, as if they had lost their queen.

Chapter 10

After we had paid all of Granny's funeral expenses, there was almost nothing left of her insurance money. So Momma had to do hard washing and ironing even more than before. I tried to help, but I couldn't seem to accomplish as much as Granny. Momma was ailing, and worried continually about my education. I was almost ready for high school, and crazy to go. I even had dreams of going to college, but that probably would never happen. We didn't even have money to send me to high school.

Minister was still boarding at our house. His three dollars a week did help, but not much. Finally, he suggested that he adopt me. He would take full responsibility for my education. Momma pondered over this a long time. She wanted me to have all the advantages I could get. But most of all, she wanted me to be a school teacher of music. So she smiled at Minister, hugged him, and then said, "Yes...without a doubt...yes. Thank you, Jesus!" Minister lifted Momma in his arms, and twirled her around the room.

The next day they went to a lawyer. The papers were drawn up. I was legally adopted by Minister Roy Franklin. Of course, this was with the understanding, I will continue to live with Momma. That I would never use his name. I thought all this was just grand. I'd never known my own father. Now I had a father like the other kids! He was a swell father, too. He said, I had to always make sure my appearance, was in keeping with his well-merited reputation. So he bought me fine clothes, and took me everywhere in town. Although, what was really wonderful, he let me sing in all the churches on Sunday mornings, and sometimes on Sunday afternoon! He'd introduce me around as his daughter. Then everybody would say, "How wonderful it is the way Minister looks after Georgie! It's a good thing Mrs. Harvey let Reverend Franklin adopt Georgie!"

More often now when Minister came home from church duties, he would say, "Come on Tutti, scratch my head, so I can go to sleep." Without a blink of hesitation, I'd stand between his knees, and scratch his head with his blue comb. Then he'd grab me all at once, and hold his mouth to mine... suddenly pushing me away. "Run along. That's enough." Then he'd give me a couple of dollars. "Give that to your Mother. It'll help her." It sure did! Momma was so delighted to get the money. Her whole face would light up, like a million lights. I was extremely happy that Minister was so kind to me and Momma. I began to call him "Uncle."

When school was out in June, Uncle said to Momma, "Lucy, I've got to go down to south east Missouri for my conferences. I'll be gone for three or four weeks. Since it's so hot here, and much cooler down there, I thought it would be nice for Georgie to come with me, and have a little vacation. Anyway, there's nothing for her to do here."

Momma was so happy for me to go. "It'll be a great thing for you to be able to have a real vacation, just like white kids have!" She got all my little things together in a chip basket with a handle. She hugged me tightly for a moment, then she looked at me with her warm brown eyes, as she held both of my hands. "Now, you sure be a good girl, and don't go disgracing me." With a serious face, I promised Momma that I would be good, even though I could barely stand still. I was bursting inside with joy - there was no holding me. I'd never been any place in my whole life!

Momma saw us to the streetcar, then she hurried back home to work. The streetcar seemed to take hours to get to the station. Uncle was so amused that I had never been on a train before, that he became excited by my joy. Finally, we made it to Vanderventer Station. The train wasn't there, so we still had to wait ten more minutes. Uncle started gently kneading my shoulders, because I was getting lightheaded from all the anticipation.

When the train crawled into the station, I was crazy to get on board. But Uncle said, "Wait a minute. I want to see what conductor is on." I stood with large shinning eyes looking, and worshipping that big monster train. I was honest-to-goodness going to travel! We got on, and went into one of the fine coaches. I held my nose so high, you couldn't see it. I thought - now the other kids haven't anything on me!

The conductor came through, and Uncle knew him! Uncle said, "This is my daughter, Chief. I'm taking her down to the country for a vacation." The conductor took my hand, raised it to his lips, and kissed the air about a half-inch above my gloved fingers. I near burst with pride. "Hope you have a good time," and he went on down the aisle.

"Don't you have to pay?"

"I don't have to pay, because I have traveled so long up and down this road, everybody knows me." Wasn't it like a make-believe story to be Uncle's daughter? I felt like a princess, as I sensed his pride in me.

The man came through with baskets of peanuts, popcorn, bananas, and soda water. Uncle loaded me down with all of the treats. It was better than any story or even a picnic. The train pulled into one station, where there were old ladies with big baskets of fried chicken, homemade cakes, and pies. Uncle bought some of everything for our lunch. I was so extremely happy, that I just cuddled up warmly in his arms.

"When we get to Poplar Bluff, we will stay at Sister Carrie's. She's a widow-woman like your mother, and has two little boys about your age…just going on fourteen, I think. I always stay there to help her out, same as I do with your mother. Sister Carrie has three rooms, and I have the large front room…." I didn't hear any more, because I fell fast asleep.

The next thing I remember, Uncle was shaking me. "Wake up. We're almost there." I jumped up full of excitement again, washed my face, then stood at the door ready to get off. It was night, so I couldn't see nothing, excepting moving darkness, and sudden bright lights. The train lurched to a quick stop, and Uncle helped me off. He looked around, "Oh…there's Brother Sims."

"Hello, Elder." A puffy face man with stooped shoulders smiled, and waved at us.

"Brother Simms, this is my daughter, Georgie," Uncle said in an even tone. "I brought her down for a vacation."

"That's fine… mighty fine. The children round here'll see to it she has a good time." We drove off in Brother Simms' four-seated buggy. I'd never been in such a swanky buggy - ever! Was I feeling elegant!

I couldn't see much as we drove, but this town seemed a lot smaller than St. Louis. We went up a hill. "The colored people live here, and most of the houses are very nice. Sister Carrie's house is in a big garden, and set back among shade trees," Uncle said as he hugged, but did not kiss me. He just placed his hand affectionately against my cheek. Then he continued with a smile, "Anyway, she…I mean, Sister Carrie has an immense farm, too, with fruit trees and all sorts of things on it. You'll have a fine time farming." Uncle looked down at me smiling. I was so beside myself, I couldn't talk!

We pulled up before a lovely picturesque house, and Sister Carrie came out - a different type than Momma - tall and thin. She rushed up to Uncle, and warmly shook his hand, "There you are, Elder!"

"This is my daughter, Georgie," Uncle said again in an even tone. "I brought her down for a vacation."

"I'm sure glad to have her," Sister Carrie said with a differential smile. "The boys'll be tickled. They tried to wait up, but they fell asleep."

Graciously I held out my hand, so that Sister Carrie could shake it. Instead she took me in her arms, and gave me a warm bear hug. I immediately liked her right off.

We went inside into Uncle's big room, and set my chip basket, and his large valise down. I slowly looked around. There was only one bed. I stiffened slightly. Then I forced a polite smile, and refrained from saying anything. But within seconds, I found the confidence to say in a casual voice, "Uncle, where am I going to sleep?"

"Oh... that's right," he said after a moment of silence. "Sister Carrie, please bring in the couch from your room, so as Georgie can sleep on it."

After getting the couch moved into Uncle's room, we went into the kitchen and had tea. Although, tea or not tea, I was just plain exhausted. Sister Carrie and Uncle went out on the porch to sit on the swing. I went into our room to get ready for bed.

Everything was so exciting, and mentally I wanted the night to go on and on. But it was past my bedtime, and I was so tired. I turned the coal-oil lamp down low. I undressed, put on my little unbleached muslin nightgown, got on my knees and said, "Dear God. Please make Momma and Uncle happy, and I will be a very good girl... thank you for a wonderful journey." I fell onto the couch. In a half a shake of a cat's tail, I was fast asleep.

...Somebody was shaking me slight-like. The lamp was turned down so low, it was near dark. I could hardly see Uncle, moving back across the room in his long white muslin nightshirt. Barely his bed creaked as he sat down. "I can't sleep. Come scratch my head, will you? It will help me to sleep." If he wasn't sleepy, I sure was. But I rubbed my eyes, got off the couch... I was so sleepy... it was so hot....

Uncle handed me his blue comb. I stood between his knees

as usual, and scratched his head. He held his arms around me. In a little while he said, "That's enough." I laid his blue comb on the nightstand, turned - he took my arm, pulled me to him, and grabbed me in his arms! Suddenly, he kissed me violently - kissed my face, my throat, and licked my ears. His hands rubbed all over me. He bit my lips. I pulled away. He sat there gasping.

"Uncle, you musn't do that!"

His hand snaked out and held the nape of my neck. "I won't hurt you...."

I looked down at the floor, as a mixture of shame, and embarrassment surged through me. I finally managed to say, "But Momma told me not to let boys play with my person. You're a man!"

"If you will let me love you, I'll stop your Mother from working altogether," his fingers gently squeezed the base of my head. I felt a peculiar kind of heat rush through my body. Somehow it seemed right that his fingers should be there. For the pleasure it gave Uncle...he had been so very kind. I really hadn't been good enough to him. Dear sweet Uncle. "Your Mother can rest now, Tutti. She needs it. I'll send you to college, too. I'll give you all the fine clothes you want." He stopped stroking the back of my head. His strong hand positioning me for another kiss.

But it wasn't his lips that touched me first. It was his tongue...wet and warm, and soft as velvet, it slid along my dry closed lips...making them wet, daring them to open up and take his tongue inside. At the corners of my mouth, his tongue paused for a few seconds, then it just licked my entire mouth eagerly. Uncle's eyes held mine, as he lifted my nightgown up, and reached shamelessly for my breasts. He bent his head, and his mouth closed over them. I felt my panic stricken nipples get unbelievably hard.

And now his hand was on my stomach. I was so ashamed at the fire that was raging in me. Its flames licking at my sleepiness, waking me up, as I fought against this strange emotion. Lower still, Uncle's hands reaching together, seeking, feeling for the place , which would seal us together in shame. But the shame gave way to the pleasure source. It was hot and wet, and nervous and grateful, yet frightened by the touching fingers.

His fingers had won now, and they seemed happy about my tense nipples. My helplessness...crying out to be used for this new pleasure. So I let myself go to this strange new urge. Like a tulip at the first kiss of the early morning sun, I felt myself open up to him.

Uncle smiled happily. One hand stayed where it was, the other flew gently to my lips - dry and parched with this sudden desire. Then he rested a finger on my cheek. "Tonight we'll make love."

"But…. Oooooh, Uncle…." I moaned, uncontrollably. It felt like a star burst down below. I could feel this glorious wetness oozing out of me. I felt happy that Uncle was enjoying the taste of me. He kept demanding more and more and more of me.

Then he put his thing inside of me…my mind began fading, because of the shame I felt…enjoying the pleasure of Uncle moving up and down in me. As he held me firm with his hands, I seemed to be under a spell. His eyes bore deeply into mine. Then he gave voice to the awesome feeling that raged through him.

Silently, slowly he pulled himself out of me - - With much confusion in my head, I went back to the couch on the other side of the room.

The next morning Uncle told me he was sending Momma some money. Then he went into town, and brought back two lovely dresses for me. I put them in my little chip basket, Momma had packed so neatly. I examined myself in the looking-glass. I didn't look any different since the incident. So I guessed that I was alright. I walked out on the porch, and slumped down on the swing. I felt so lackadaisical, so sort of floating and far away.

I looked into blank space, and started swinging and swinging…slowly back and forth. What was all this about? Why did Uncle tell me I must never tell anybody? I didn't feel any different towards him. I was just so puzzled. Anyway, he'd sent Momma money. Now she wouldn't have no more hard work. I decided never to tell anyone - just maybe my friend, Alice. She was married after all… she'd understand all of this.

Benny and Jimmy, Sister Carrie's boys, came along. "Georgie! Come on! Let's go blackberry picking!" All of a sudden I felt restless, and my energy returned. Blackberry picking…that sounded swell! I ran down those porch steps, my dress tail arguing with the wind. The day was beautiful…the sun was shining brightly, and everything smelled so inviting - clover, flowers, berries. I was very happy.

Three weeks later when we returned to St. Louis, Momma immediately rushed up to me, hugging very tightly. Then she stepped back from me, and carefully looked me over. "How fine you're looking! How grown-up! Did you have a good time?"

"I sure did! We went in the orchard and got peaches, and cherries right off the trees. We brought in corn and tomatoes and beans out of the garden, and I made milk into butter." I took a sip from the glass of lemonade that Momma had handed me, before twirling around the room. "And, oh, Momma, there was a church picnic! We went in a four-seated buggy! There were parties and parties! We sure had a big time!"

"Well, you must thank Uncle and be very dutiful to him, and obey him, always." She was so pleased, but she didn't look well.

"Don't you feel good, Momma?"

She smoothed her sweaty, nappy hair down with her watered wrinkled hand. "Well... no...."

"What's the matter?"

"Oh... nothing... just hard work." I nearly laughed out loud with joy, knowing she wouldn't have to work anymore. But I didn't say anything. Uncle looked at me with an indescribable flickering glow in his eyes. I smiled at him gratefully.

"Lucy, why don't you stop working for awhile?"

"I can't, Minister! I have to have money to get long on."

Uncle looked at me again. "Don't you worry, Lucy. I'll see you through."

"You're doing nough looking after Tutti."

"Well, a little more won't hurt me." From that day on, he took full responsibility of the house. He'd kept his word.

Uncle and me went across town to an old woman's house, where men and women met. It was just a plain ordinary looking house, same as any other. The old woman was gray-haired and very motherly-looking. Although she never said anything to us, excepting, "Good Morning or Good Evening"...I think it was the way she just sit there, and sipped liquor that made her seem wicked to me.

Anyway, Uncle and me would go there, and stay in a room for awhile. When we'd come back, Momma would usually be reading. She loved to read. Now she had lots of time to read, and do everything she loved.

Chapter 11

The hot days of August were full of plans for me to graduate from L'Ouverture. I was entering Sumner High School in January. Uncle happily bought me books, and school clothes. I was so crazy about one shepherd plaid dress, trimmed in black velvet, with small brass buttons, that every time I looked at it, I wanted to scream! It was longer than any dress I'd ever worn. Soon I'd be wearing real long dresses, and putting my hair up. I was fourteen, and sure growing up.

A vacancy opened up in St. Paul's choir on a Tuesday. By Sunday Morning Services, everyone kept saying, "Georgie, you have such a beautiful voice. Why don't you join?" I sure wanted to get that opportunity of singing before one thousand, five hundred people every Sunday. I loved singing more than anything. I was nervous all that day just thinking about it...I was probably too young. Then late the next afternoon, Choirmaster asked me to join. Everything was just so swell. I could barely hold myself together to eat dinner. Even Momma and Uncle had a hard time containing their joy.

The first night of rehearsal in the big lecture room was most thrilling. All the singers stood ramrod straight and tried to outdo each other in a bright, cheerful, optimistic way. Meanwhile, the Choirmaster quietly made notes on a card.

I was placed with the contraltos and had new songs to learn - anthems, hymns. I sang with all my soul, my voice ringing out, until I forgot everything. I was just a mighty sound. When we finished, it was like coming back from a vision.

All the people in the choir were older than me. So I'd never met any of them before. I sat next to a man named Henry. He was a young widower that had nice ways. Just a nice comfortable Saint Bernard looking man in his late twenties. Even though he had pudgy cheeks, he had a pretty good baritone voice. He took to seeing me home. After a few weeks, I grew to like him a lot.

Each time I song in that wonderful large church, I thought back to Black Patti's performance - the queenly way she looked in her long white dress. How she had travelled all over, because of her singing. That's what I wanted. So I worked hard and learned all the songs. In one month, I was made soloist.

Every Sunday morning, all of the churches had "Opening the Doors of the Church," to get people to join. The whole choir would sing. But when I sang my big solo, as many as fifty people at one time joined church. People would even call the church to ask if I was going to sing. I discovered the vibrating excitement of standing before a big audience. I'd make the audience feel every inch of my joy. It was being one with them. But at the same moment being free, far, and way above everyone else.

Chapter 12

I entered Sumner High School full of enthusiasm. There was Latin, Algebra, Chemistry, Rhetoric, English Literature, and Domestic Science - new, fascinating things. I liked Chemistry, and English Literature the best. So I organized a Literary Society for debating. Then a Glee Club, which got famous for singing at school exercises. We were even invited all over to sing at church concerts.

It all made me feel like I was completely grown up. Until I discovered the railroad, just behind our house, ran one block away from Sumner. That automatically pleased me. So my favourite method of getting to school, which was twenty blocks from home, became "car-hopping" - catching the back-down of a passing blind railroad coach. Hanging on for dear life…it was swift, exciting, and didn't cost a cent.

There were other things that assured me that I wasn't exactly a grown-up lady, too. Like sliding down the school banisters were more fun than hopping trains. Of course, that was until I slid right into the principal's arms. Before I realized it, Momma came bearing down on me, thrashing me real good again.

Then the day the circus came to town, my best friend Beatrice, and me ran away from school. We just had to hear the calliope. One time we stayed out, and went to see "McFadden's Flats." It was such a funny show with white people acting. It was the first play I'd ever seen. It was a new world. The most fascinating world I'd ever seen. For days after that, I went around pretending to be the people in the show. There were all these things, and many more to prove I was still little Tutti Harvey, "the brat!"

Chapter 13

About three months after I entered school, I began to feel sick all the time. I couldn't keep anything on my stomach. Almost anything made me sick…any type of smell would seem to spiral deep into my stomach, then come up immediately as vomit. Along with the sickness, my head seemed to spin around. So I'd walk around dizzy, almost every morning.

One day at my friend Alice's house, one of those spells came on. I tried to hide it, but Alice saw something was wrong. She leaned forward in her chair, "What's the matter, Georgie?"

"I don't know," I stood slumped against the wall. "I feel this way all the time, especially every time I eat."

She got up, and stood next to me, "Is anything else wrong?" Alice's big brown eyes grew larger as she stared at me.

I looked down at the floor, as tears streamed down my cheeks. I didn't know what to say. I just collapsed onto the couch, wiping beads of sweat from my forehead.

"Georgie," Alice frowned, "have you been doing things you shouldn't do?"

I looked at Alice's black hair, which was set in the new pompadour style. She was always so lady-like…so neat…so properly married. All of a sudden, I was so ashamed…so humiliated…water seem to overflow from my stinging eyes, as I blurted out the whole story.

"Georgie, I can hardly believe it! You better go right home, and tell the Minister, or your mother may find out!"

That nearly scared me to death. Momma would sure kill Uncle! I didn't know what to do. I couldn't understand how Uncle could do such a thing to me? How he could make so much trouble?

Alice hugged me warmly. Then she sat next to me, and pressed her face against my cheek. "Don't worry," she said with a marginal bit of enthusiasm, "you just tell the Minister. He'll fix it so nobody will ever know."

When I got home, Momma was ironing some of my pretty new dresses. Uncle wasn't there. I sat down not facing Momma, fearful that she would see me shivering with sickness and chills. I though of places I could go for a visit, until Uncle got back. If I stayed too long, Momma would notice that I was weak.

"Tutti, go down and bring up a scuttle of coal." That was a pleasure. I ran to the cellar door...happy to get away from Momma...afraid she might suspect something. I raced down a step, my heel caught...falling...smashing, crashing down the whole length of the stairs! Misery filled every part of me. I just laid there screaming...weeping...the hurt...the awful pain in my side. Momma rushed downstairs with Uncle following her.

"My, God...." Momma began to cry, as she braced my head against her arm. "My baby...my baby."

"Lucy, you stay here," Uncle said, as he bent down and picked me up. "Go on with your work. I'll take Tutti to the doctor."

We went to the streetcar, and rode awhile without either one of us saying a word. I was so ashamed, and humiliated. I didn't know how to express myself, but finally I mumbled, "Uncle, I got something to tell you. I feel sick all the time, especially when I eat. I...."

Just as I could feel Momma's strong motherly love. I now felt the exact opposite from Uncle. It was like a chill oozed from him, as he grew hostile. "Have you been playing with other boys?"

"Certainly not!" I was so upset about him asking me about other boys. I just wanted to stand straight up, and whack him across his face.

"Well, I can't take you to your Mother's doctor." Uncle's voice was so condescending, that it seem to pick up a ball of dirt from the floor of the street car, and turn it into slimy mud. "I'll take you to a doctor I know."

We got off the streetcar, with me leaning carefully next to Uncle, so I didn't appear to be sick, and walked immediately into some white man's office. He examined me carefully. "She's pregnant...about three months."

Tears filled my eyes, and trickled down my cheeks...I silently cried...so ashamed that I bowed my head in despair. Yet, it was true. I was going to have a baby. They would throw me out of church. I couldn't sing any more. Momma would kill the Minister. I almost cried until I couldn't see or hear anything. But the doctor told me, "Don't worry. We'll fix everything all right. Nobody'll ever know." He gave me some white capsules. Then me and Uncle went home.

"What did the doctor say?" Momma wanted to know the moment we walked in the door. "I know," she nervously rubbed her water wrinkled hands together, "...is she - "

Uncle cut her off with a wave of his hand, as if to say, "I told you I'd take care of everything." Then he held Momma's hand, and gently said, "I took her to a white doctor I knew, and he said she only wrenched her side."

Momma looked very confused, as she pulled her hand away from Uncle's, as if he had a rare disease. "Wrenched her side." She sighed heavily.

"You musn't worry, Lucy," Uncle tried to comfort Momma by placing his arm around her. "It's really nothing dangerous, and Tutti will be all right in a few days." He dropped wearily down onto the sofa, and picked up the Bible from the end table. "Believe...praise God...the Lord will take care. It's just a little storm in a teacup, Lucy...no harm done."

Two days later, I was determined to conceal my panic, on the way to the doctor's office. When I looked frightened, it made Uncle so upset that he would sometimes shake like a leaf. I was afraid he might have a heart attack or something. So I forced myself to keep calm. This way I would get the proper medicine to cure my sickness.

The doctor didn't examine me this time. He simply gave me a brownish, bitter medicine. "Be sure, Reverend, you're around her all the time. As soon as she feels a cramp, bring her straight to me. Anything can happen."

About thirty-six hours later, while I was standing at our front gate, to get away from the smell of cooking...dizziness...so dizzy that people walking by looked like they were far-off swaying shapes. A sharp pain struck me - my belly! - My back! The pain was like a shearing hot fireplace poker ripping across my insides...it jolted me...nearly caused me to fall down. I called to Uncle, who was sitting in the window seat. "My side hurts...my God the pain!" He rushed downstairs with Momma following directly behind him.

I was sure Momma suspected something, as she held me in her arms. "It's all right...my Lord...my baby." She shot Uncle a warning look, "maybe, I better go with you?"

"No," Uncle gently took me out of Momma's arms. "You go back and finish fixing dinner."

She hesitated for a moment. "All right...as long as you

know that's my only child." She blew her nose on one of the lace handkerchiefs, I had given her. Then she added unsteadily, "But find out why those pains are so severe. Perhaps, Tutti's broken a rib."

Uncle was so anxious to get to the doctor's office, he didn't bother to answer Momma. He just rushed out with me, gazing helplessly at him.

The old thin doctor, who looked shrunken in his big white medical coat, asked me to lay on the table. "You just stay here quiet." I laid there about three quarters of an hour - then another sudden sharp pain hit me!

"Doctor! Oh...my God...Doctor!" I screamed at the top of my voice, as blood gushed between my legs.

"You're all right now," the doctor said, in a soothing voice. "You don't have to worry anymore." The nurse cleaned me up, while she instructed me about how to care for myself. Then the doctor fixed me up with white gaze packing, taped my side, and Uncle took me home.

Momma looked up from the book she was reading at my wrapped side. "I knew your rib was broken," Momma's voice was calm. "I just thank God you're all right."

"It isn't broken," I looked down, away from her. I was not only ashamed, but I looked so awful standing there with holes in my stockings, and stains all over my bright yellow dress. "But...Momma, I bruised myself. I'll have to lay in bed for about a week, and wear this taping to support me."

"You sure should be grateful for having such a fine man like Uncle to look after you." Momma said, she was near crying with gratitude. "I don't know what we'd do without him."

With the doctor's medicine, I mended within a week. I was glad to be back at church, and school, singing, learning new, and interesting things. After all that had happened, I never allowed Uncle to touch me again.

Although he pleaded and begged, "I'll withdraw my support from your mother, and you. She'll have to do hard work again!" It was never the same. I'd always respond tersely with, "If you do that, I'll tell her what you've done to me, and she'll kill you!" He'd leave me alone for awhile, even though he kept nagging and begging. I hated him.

Chapter 14

We still had "Music Hour" in school. That was when the "Music Man" came and taught us different scales and exercises. I loved that type of singing. I considered it real singing. It never occurred to me to practice the scales at home. Singing wasn't anything, I had to do like homework. It was just the same as breathing or eating - something I did because I loved it. Something I just had to do.

Ada Overton, a St. Louis girl I knew, went to New York to visit a friend. While there she was able to get into a real show called "In Dahomey," which was run by Williams and Walker. They were a most famous colored team, who produced musical comedies surrounding their humorous songs. Ada wrote telling me that with my voice, I should have no trouble getting in a show. That was okay with me. I was so crazy to be in shows, and sing to lots of people - even more than at church. I just wanted to travel all over the world like Black Patti.

In fact after seeing Black Patti perform, I'd spend hours dreaming about my success. I was going to be like one of those fancy horseless carriages. Only I would never breakdown. My carriage would be one of nerve, imagination, flexibility, hard work, and the knack for making friends...my fancy singing carriage wouldn't breakdown anywhere.

William and Walker came to St. Louis, and Ada got them to invite me over. I put on my best imitation gold bracelets, and flew over there. George Walker was a god to me. He'd originated the strut, and was known everywhere. I took one look at him, and knew he must be a god. He had a beautiful loud-checkered suit on, and diamonds - real flashy! Even Ada, who was now George's wife, had big diamond hoops in her ears!

After I sang one number for them, they wanted to take me right along with the show. So I rushed home to tell Momma. She just listened, then slowly raised her eyes to mine, and said, "No!" Then she quietly looked down at her book, and continued to read. She looked up at me again, "I mean it, Tutti. You can't go. You have to finish school."

When Mr. Walker heard that he laughed. "That's all right, Georgie. You go learn a lot," he paused. His light brown eyes seemed unnaturally clear. When he looked straight into my eyes, I found it impossible to turn away. "Anyway, Georgie," he smiled widely, "you'll be coming to New York one of these days, don't you worry. Come round see the show tonight."

I was so excited, I couldn't utter a single word. I mean, going to the show, was almost as good as going with them.

That night I saw my first musical show. It was glittering. So elegant, I could scarce think! Mr. Walker sang "Castle on the River Nile," and Bert Williams - "I Ain't Done Nothing to Nobody." Ada Walker sang "Hannah from Savannah." A young girl named Chic danced and sang like she was joy itself!

They all wore beautiful, shining, shortish dresses. Their dresses were actually showing their legs, up to their knees! I thought them so naughty! It wasn't quite right for grown women to traipse around in short dresses. But wouldn't I just love to be doing it.

After the musical was over, I sat in my seat for a moment. I just stared at the curtain. I was just that overwhelmed by the glamour, and wonderful songs in the show. Finally, after it seemed like everyone had left, I went around the back to the stage door.

Then to my delight, Ada held my hand, as she introduced me to everybody in the show. They were so pleased to see me. There was such good cheer, laughing and happy shouting. I knew that I'd never forget the excitement...most of all, I knew right then and there that I had to get into a show. Even if the women did wear naughty dresses.

When I went to school the next day, I was the envy of all the kids. I acted out everything I'd seen. So all the kids were sure, I had to get in a show, too.

Senior year was really one of my best. I was made class president. I, also, had an oration, and a solo. I was eighteen, and Momma was so proud of me. She even went out, and bought me some white satin graduation shoes! That was something I'd wanted, ever since I'd seen Black Patti's. I could hardly keep them off my feet. I loved them so much!

I had lots of flowers, too, from choir friends and Alice - carnations, red roses. Choir-mistress furnished my carriage, but Uncle - who had promised to give me my graduation dress and fan - refused to give them. I didn't tell Momma he hadn't bought them. He didn't tell her either. He did not attend my graduation exercises. He had taken to walking around in circles, mumbling biblical verses.

Chapter 15

Two years before my high school graduation, Henry, the widower had asked me to marry him. After several choir rehearsals, and many church services, he took to seeing me home. He, also, escorted me to places - parties, church socials. Everybody thought of him as my steady company. I liked him, but I didn't think that I loved him.

Every time Henry saw me home or took me out, Uncle made a terrible scene. He didn't want me to even talk to any boys. He was so insanely jealous that it was unbelievable. Several times with his fists angrily clenched, he screamed at Henry. Telling him that he was without good Christian morals. How his lusting after me was evil. As much as I tried, I couldn't make Uncle act decent. Finally, out of desperation, Uncle asked me to sit with him on the porch. Then he had the nerve to ask me to marry him.

"I would rather die and go to hell first, than marry you!" I almost yelled at him, before rushing back into the house. He got so upset by all of this, that he became sick. Spending a lot of his day in bed, talking about Jezebel.

Henry kept asking me to marry him, too, and I - really praying, that something would free me from Uncle - didn't dare tell Henry what had happened to me. Besides, there was the everlasting nagging threat - Uncle would withdraw his support, and Momma would have to go back to washing and ironing.

Between Uncle threatening, and Henry begging me to marry him...things took such an unbearable turn that I was always in a state of confusion. So I decided to just tell Henry everything. If he wanted me after he knew, all right.

"Want you!" He held me tenderly, "Of course, I want you. I'll kill him. I'll tell your mother."

"You mustn't do any of those things, Henry," I pulled him towards the couch. "Just be calm. Try to forget it. Soon as we can, we'll get married."

Now Henry was with me more than ever, but I didn't mind. The real truth of the matter, was that I had just met a man that I felt free to tell my most inner secrets...at a time when I felt desperate. Henry held out a light of hope in those dark crazy days of my life.

Uncle watched us continually, and went from sipping gin to

drinking heavy. Soon he started staying in bed night and day with heart trouble and Bright's disease.

One night Momma went out to visit a friend, leaving me alone with Uncle. As soon as he felt she'd really left, he called me to his bed. "I just plain don't understand," he said between coughing, "how you could behave privately in such a way with Henry."

I grimaced, but said nothing. The only sounds in the room was the chirping coming from Momma's caged canaries.

"You say you're going to marry Henry," Uncle asked after what seemed like a very long pause.

"Yes."

Uncle stroked his gray goatee. He started coughing and clearing his throat. "I intended you should marry me when I get well," he said in a voice that was growing weaker with each word. Then his entire body began to jerk for about a minute of wretched coughing.

Finally, after his spasm stopped, I said quietly, "I told you once, I'd rather die first than marry you."

He gazed up at me puzzled. His eyes were tired, and had a tortured expression. All of a sudden, he looked terribly old and thin to me. "Does Henry know about you?" he asked in a weak surly manner.

"If you have any idea of telling him anything, you need not waste words. I've told him everything."

Uncle just rolled over with his back to me. But I could tell from the shaking of his frail shoulders, he was crying. From that moment on, life seemed to go out of him, and he went down, down. A week later, he died. Momma cried a whole lot, because he'd been such a good kind man. So very helpful to me.

He was buried from St. Paul's church. He was known as a great worker for the Lord - having built many churches, and saved many from going under the auctioneer's hammer. Four important fellow clergymen carried his casket. They placed him under a marble Bible which was inscribed in medium letters, "HE RESTS FROM HIS LABOURS, AND HIS WORKS DO FOLLOW HIM."

Chapter 16

Dr. Roberts of St. Paul's married me to Henry Mickey, three days after Uncle had been buried. I still didn't really love Henry. I respected, admired, and thought more of him than any other man. Also, he had shown me the way out of an unbearable situation.

Working in the railroad yard, cleaning out cars, gave Henry enough money to pay our rent, and household expenses. I was making a little money, too, singing at local teas. It all helped to keep Momma from hard work. Since it was cheaper for all of us to live in one house, Henry and his son, Maurice, came to live with us.

Three mornings after we were married, I woke up to find Henry still sleeping. It was six o'clock. If he didn't get up, he'd be late for work. I shook him.

"What's matter?" He groaned, sinking his head deeper into the pillow.

"Time to get up."

"I don't feel like getting up..."

I studied his face for a moment, "don't you feel good?"

"I'm all right...just don't feel like working today. I'm tired."

"You may be tired, but you got to get up and go work. You got to keep your job!"

Henry turned towards me, stretching like a sleepy hound dog. "Well, honey," he glared at me, "you're singing at three teas this week - "

My eyes collided with his, "what's that got to do with your working? I didn't marry you to help you take care of me!"

"Martha used to work and help make a living," his nostrils flared angrily.

By now I was standing with my hands defiantly on my hips. "What Martha did I don't intend to do! If you feel that way about it, go back to your mother! I don't need you!"

Henry rose up out of the bed with daggers in his eyes, and pulled his clothes on. "That is just what I'm going to do!" He stamped out.

I hurriedly threw my things on, and rushed over to Dr. Roberts. I didn't need Henry's help. In a few days, I'd sure have the property Uncle must have left me. I wouldn't have to worry about no drudgery. I ran into the parsonage.

"Dr. Roberts, I have left Henry Mickey!"

He took off his horn-rimmed glasses, and rubbed the welts on the bridge of his nose. "But I just married you."

"Well, Henry had dropped his job, and wants me to work!"

"Oh, you can patch that up between you. Go on back home." That's just what I didn't want to hear. "Although, since you're here, sit down a minute." He went over to his desk, and took a long envelope out.

"Your Uncle gave this to me about a month ago." Dr. Roberts held up a big, folded paper. Then he put his glasses back on, and read lots of uninteresting, legal-sounding words - most of which I didn't understand. At last, "- All my property and personal belongings, I bequeath" - that's what I wanted to hear! - "To my Cousin..." I didn't listen no more. It was just like Uncle to do this to us. Now I'd have to go backwards. I'd have to work - wash, and iron like Momma. The telephone rang, and Dr. Roberts politely said, "Yes...yes...she's here. She's on her way home right now."

Things finally settled down after that, and a mundane daily routine set in. I didn't really know if this was suppose to be good or bad. I was just going through the motions of being a housewife.

Then one day while Henry was at work, Maurice was out on the porch, making as much noise as he could playing, and I was singing, to keep from being bored, while I cleaned, there was a firm knock on the door.

"Is Henry Mickey here?" A fat, balding man asked.

"No, but I'm his wife. What do you want?"

The jowly man straightened his well-worn tie, then announced flatly, "I read the marriage license in the newspaper, and came to collect the money your husband owes us."

"For what?"

"For his first wife's funeral."

Well, that was a hell of an answer. I shuddered at the morbid thought. I was tempted to say, "I didn't marry her." But instead I said, "Henry isn't here now... really... but you come back when he is."

I pulled on a warm sweater to protect me from the shivers, running up and down my spine, and went for a walk. Why was it so hard for Dr. Roberts, and Momma to understand I didn't want this marriage. It just wasn't working between Henry and me. I was so upset about the direction of my life…about my singing. I don't even remember where I had walked, or how long I had been walking…twenty minutes, half an hour, maybe. After my astonishing conversation, with that ugly fat man, about Henry's wife funeral expenses, I needed to be by myself. I needed to untangle my thoughts, and my muddled feelings about my unwanted marriage.

The next morning, a tall, stooped, thin man inquired for Henry.

"What do you want?" I blurted out, without giving the man a chance to say why he wanted Henry.

"I came to collect on the wedding ring your husband purchased."

Words died in my mouth. "Ain't that paid for either?" I finally managed to ask.

He shook his head, and his eyes flicked down away from mine. "It ain't."

I willed myself to keep calm. "You be sure to come back later when Henry'll be here."

Shortly after that Maurice decided to chop our furniture up. So he took his toy hatchet, and proceeded to hack at our brand new dressing-case. Momma immediately snatched the hatchet away. Maurice didn't like that at all. He simply laid on the floor, and yelled so loud with rage, that I rushed indoors. "What on earth's the matter?"

"You know, Georgie," Momma paused, sipping her coffee for a moment, "charity is not just giving a dog a bone. It is giving a dog a bone when you are as hungry as the dog. I believe in the good Lord. I believe in charity, but…"

We looked at each other for a second, "Yes, all of that is true, Momma."

"Maurice was chopping on the new dresser," Momma continued between sips of coffee, "so, I took his horrible hatchet away."

I put my arm around Momma's shoulders. "That's okay," I said, holding her tightly. "It was a good thing you did. I mean, afterall…."

Maurice continued to bellow louder and louder, kicking his feet up and down, and banging his fists on the floor.

I both heard and felt Momma's horrified gasp as Henry

flung open the door. Without even looking at us, he rushed over to Maurice. "What's the matter, son? I heard you yelling down the street."

"Mis' Harvey hit me!" It sounded like Momma had killed him.

"I didn't touch Maurice at all," Momma said quietly. "He was chopping the furniture, so I took his hatchet away."

"Sit down, Henry," I said, motioning him towards a chair. "Momma's right. She didn't hurt Maurice."

Maurice almost choked with fury. "She did hit me!"

"You know you're lying, Maurice!" I fought to control a scream. "She didn't touch you! Henry, you wouldn't take this child's word against Momma's?"

"She could be lying well as Maurice." He was still focused on Maurice. He never even looked at us. "I mean... I just came from work. I don't know who's lying!"

A chilling silence fell on the room for a second. I looked at Momma, and she looked at me - it was over. Then I threw the hatchet at Henry, but it didn't hit him. "Take your darn brat, and get out!" They rushed for the door. I was so fit to be tied. I screamed after them, "You found me here! You can leave me here!"

The next morning I packed their things; took them to Henry's mother's; threw them on her doorstep; rang the bell, and ran back home. After that I didn't hear from Henry for about a month. One of the men in the choir said, he was down South visiting his father. I didn't care much where he had gone. I was singing at lots of teas for white people. I was just happy that I was making enough money to carry Momma and me.

Walking home from choir rehearsal one night, Henry stepped out of a dark doorway near my house. I wasn't surprised.

"What do you want, Henry Mickey?"

"I want to talk to you." He was very quiet-like.

"Fire away."

"I want to make up and come back," Henry said, smiling that charming smile of his that was so irresistible. "I promise to work, and I'll leave Maurice with my mother."

I didn't really truly want Henry back, but we were married. Finally, I consented.

Chapter 17

Singing at teas gave me the opportunity for more people to hear me, and talk about my voice. So when the 1903 St. Louis Exposition opened, I sang for all sorts of events. This time I made more money than ever before.

My voice got deeper and bassier without my trying to make it deep. People were so amazed by its depth that they would sit in astonishment after my performances. Henry's jealousy grew worst, the more I was admired.

While I was singing "Holy City" - my special big number - for the General Conference of the African Methodist Episcopal Zion Church, Bishop Waters heard me. After I turned to thank the Bishop for an inspiring message, courtesies were exchanged, and we both agreed that the weather was dreadful, "But it was your wonderful voice that brought us the sunshine, Georgette." The Bishop held my hand for a brief moment, as if he were receiving a blessing from me, before he continued, "We're having a conference in Louisville, Kentucky. Would you like to sing for us there?"

Louisville was an overnight train ride. I'd never song away from home, nor rode on a train all night. "I sure would!" I smiled, radiantly. "Thank you... thank you very much!" I flew home to tell Momma, but I didn't think nothing about Henry. I was sick, and tired of his chilling expressions of jealousy. I wasn't studying about him. He had conniptions.

"You're not going!"

I was so startled by him, trying to verbally block my new success, that it took me a moment to answer. "I sure am," I said, suddenly becoming very businesslike. "I know I have to work for Momma, and me to survive. You don't believe in working."

"Oh, I see," Henry bit his bottom lip, before subsiding into a puzzled silence. He had no idea, not even a clue, as to how to deal with me as a woman or an artist. Finally, he went outside - happiness was not the word. I needed room. I needed to catch my breath, so that I could prepare for my singing engagement. Afterall, I was going to be the next "Black Patti."

Louisville was a beautiful place. For a Southern town, it had less colored prejudices, than any town I'd ever heard of - even

St. Louis. The colored people were charming, and had lovely homes. They called themselves "race members": a title blacks used to refer to themselves, at the turn of the Twentieth Century, to incite pride in people of color.

I stayed with a school teacher - a large church woman. She reminded me of a Sunday school teacher that we used to have at St. Paul's. I smiled to myself, as I thought back to the time, when I was a little girl. Paradise was suppressing laughter in church, while I tried to make Alice giggle at the wrong moment.

The night of my concert, I put on my white satin shoes, that Momma had given me for my graduation. My white organdy dress, which was so grand, was without a doubt, most like Black Patti's. My heart thumped with excitement. As I looked at myself, in the triple looking-glass, in the bedroom, I was completely elated. I only wished that I had long white gloves, tight all the way up my arm. Although, I'd for sure get those later. I just had to! Anyway, my hair was styled into a pompadour just like Black Patti's.

The church was packed, but I wasn't scared. The people were just like St. Louis people. Although, their church was smaller. So I simply said to myself, "Lord, give me success," and added, "in my first effort away from home."

Bishop Waters introduced me in grand style, and they all clapped real hard. It was just like being Black Patti, and singing in a theatre! I bowed, smiled brightly, clasped my hands in front of me, and sang. "Holy City" stood them right up demanding encore after encore. Then everybody crowded around, hoping I'd come back soon. After that we had strawberry ice cream. I felt like I was some strange new wonderful girl, I'd heard people talk about!

When I left for St. Louis, the next morning, I was twenty-five dollars richer. My entire being was in such a whirl…such euphoria. Now I was absolutely determined to sing, and travel further and further.

At home Henry was still puffed up. However, I wasn't thinking on him. I gave Momma twenty dollars, and with the other five got me some things. It was so satisfying to feel I could earn money. Not only where people knew me, but in places where I wasn't known. But most of all, was the satisfaction of knowing I could make a living by singing. That put me pert on top of the world.

A neighborhood boy, who looked like a cartoon character,

that talked in a slow Southern drawl, came to ask me to travel, and sing with "The Alabama Jubilee Singers." It was a Jubilee Company he'd formed like the Hall Johnson Singers or the Fisk Jubilee Singers. The boy's company had ten singers, and a great reputation.

"Where you going?" Henry asked, his long fingers scratching through his tightly curled hair.

"South East Missouri for two months," I said happily, as I packed my bag. "We're playing Chateauxs. You know…places where white people go to rest, and gain knowledge in the summer. They're run by churches, and have lectures, and concerts for educational relaxation. Plays aren't allowed. They're confabulations of the devil!"

Henry continued scratching his head, "this big Lyceum Bureau send you out?"

"Yes." I smiled, easily. "We want you to sing solo for fifteen dollars a week and expenses!" I couldn't even believe it myself. One hundred and twenty dollars for eight weeks of traveling around!"

"I sure would go." This time Henry consented without much arguing. But he knew I was going anyway.

Four days later, I put on a favourite pink shirtwaist, and skirt. It was an outfit that was very much my style. I looked like the airbrushed perfection of youth. This made me feel wonderful when I departed for the station. The "Alabama Jubilee Singers" were all there, lolling about. I couldn't believe my eyes though. They were all people I knew! Not one was from Alabama! My own pianist was even playing for them!

All the singers just stood around, and didn't even seem to think anything unusual was happening. They acted just kind of anxious to start, but weren't especially thrilled. Of course, they had all been away before. However, I was sure, no matter how many times I'd go away, I'd be excited. When the train finally arrived, we all got in the day coach. I felt like I was in an exciting holiday party. But everybody else, though happy and pleasant, still didn't show any special enthusiasm.

The first stop was Carthage, Missouri, and the white Minister was waiting. "Hello there, everybody!" He said, as if talking to his flock, who had came in from the wilderness. "I'm glad to see you. The bus is right over here."

We drove through the town, which was even more beautiful

than Louisville. Huge trees with branches overlapping formed perfect arcades down the streets. Everywhere we rode, people stood applauding, and all the town kids ran along besides the bus shouting, "Hello! Hello!" The singers bowed most grandly, and I did, too. It was all so wonderful - like being on a mountain of ecstasy!

When we got to the Chateaux, where we were to live and sing, I was totally taken by it all. The large clean-looking white buildings that stood all around, the playgrounds, a lake with boats, and people - young and old - swimming! A large dining room building was pointed out, too. My eyes and nose could scarce take in the colour, the clean smell of the green shrubbery, along with the bright yellow, orange, and gold-coloured flowers everywhere.

"Oh, this is what paradise must be like," exclaimed one of the sopranos, echoing my thoughts exactly.

There were a lot of white people sitting in all this clean beauty. Most of them prim in white linen dresses, and seersucker suits. As we passed by them, they bowed so friendly saying, "We are very pleased to have you all with us, and know we are all going to have a lovely singing." It made me feel like a Sunday School Bible Queen. I stuck my bosom out, and walked stiff with my noise pert!

The house we were to live in was large, white, framed, and had nine bedrooms, with a sitting room that was furnished beautifully. A piano was in this sitting room - looking very grand. However, we didn't see any dining room. "Where we going to eat?" The piano player asked the Minister.

"In the dining room with the rest of us." He smiled graciously, as his green eyes twinkled. That was a swell surprise, and an entire new experience. None of us had ever eaten in the same dining room with large groups of white people before. It turned out to be the same as eating with our own people.

That night we rehearsed, and the next afternoon was our first concert. We sang "The Bullfrog On The Bank" and "Little David Play On Your Harp." Then I sang solo. The white people, even the children, sat quiet and deeply attentive. When I finished, they clapped harder than in Louisville. But it was their looks, their postures, and their smiles, that let me know they thoroughly enjoyed my performance. Then one by one, they said what a deep, unusual, beautiful voice I had. How I should be thankful God had given it to me. That settled my future definitely. I was sure I could make a living traveling and singing. That was what I plan to do!

After two weeks of quiet and happiness, we were on our way. Although as the bus carried us to the train station, it dawned on me that there was a jagged crack in all of this bliss. The white people, who lived in Carthage, didn't simply ignore the ugly sides of life such as segregation, poverty, or war; they prettied them up. Poverty and segregation was made picturesque; war became a matter of glorious charges and pathetic deaths - but not the agonies or mutilations, I had read about in school.

I took a breath, steering my thoughts back to the present, as the bus came to a stop in front of the train station. Gathering my luggage, I rushed to join the others boarding. After we were settled in our seats, the porter saw that we were a company.

"Where you all going?"

"Monette." That was our first one night stand.

"Well, for God's sake," the porter paused to reorganize his thoughts. Finally, he said, "You don't wanna go there! Jus been a lynching! All the colored've been run out!"

I stiffened, and swallowed hard. "...Run out?"

"Yep..." the porter stopped to stare out the window. Then he looked shakened, "the horror of it all is that there ain't no other station 'fore Monette!"

For a moment, I couldn't speak...I was stunned. I felt a queasiness form in the pit of my stomach. "Well...we'll just have to get off there and see what happens."

"We'll stay close to the train." The piano player said nervously, his hands trembling.

Fear gripped the cartoon-looking face of the founder of "The Alabama Jubilee Singers." "If there are signs of fury," John cleared his throat, "we'll get right on again."

"Lynching's some bad thing," the porter shook his head, "specially, when them white folks got blood in their heads, no holding 'em!"

We all sat solemn, quiet - thinking of people being burnt alive, stoned, hanged for just being black. We all knew of many such happenings...terrified by the evil nightmares.

My mind drifted back to Granny and her slave friends. The horror stories they used to tell. One slave talked about how as a little bitty fellow - five years old - he watched a slave rushing by, where he was playing with some other slave children. The slave's hand had been cut off, and blood was dripping from it. The white people were so cruel, they not only cut his hand off, they stuck the thumb of the severed hand in the slave's mouth.

As the train slowly pulled into the station, the steam engine sounded as if it was moaning. We stood bunched together at the door, peering out. Everything looked peaceful, but we still said nothing. We just stayed clustered together, looking around anxiously.

The uncomfortable silence lasted for some time. But at last the Minister, a slim man, walked forward to greet us. "I suppose you heard about what has happened here, but don't worry. You will be perfectly safe." He smiled warmly, and sounded most cheerful and so confident.

Doubtfully, we looked at one another, around us again, and up. Our attention got glued to one spot. A rough wooden sign, seeming as if it had just been nailed, blazed, 'NIGGER DON'T LET THE SUN GO DOWN ON YOU IN THIS TOWN!'

The Minister said tranquilly, "Don't mind that," and led us into town. We all kept close after him. After all, he was a Man of God. No harm could come to him. God wouldn't let it.

We went through the downtown district. Into several large stores, where the white proprietors received us cordially. People in the streets smiled at us, too. It didn't seem like anything unusual had happened. But the hot heavy summer air seemed to drench us. So we eagerly went to the parsonage, where we were to stay until morning. We didn't leave that place for the rest of the day. We knew about lynching, and we weren't trusting nothing.

That night the concert place was packed with white people - not a colored person present, excepting us. Yet, with all of the pressure about lynching, we were still a success. To this day I don't think any colored live in Monette - only a place built by the railroad company for the colored porters.

At the grand dinner, in the church after the concert, the white people ate with us, and were lovely. The Minister embarked on some long Bible story. We had to force ourselves to pay attention to him, in between tasty bites. They didn't say one word about the lynching. But we were still very ill at ease. We just wanted to get out of Monette, as soon as possible.

We walked across the grounds, eating the strawberries, in silence, that they had given us for desert. As we got closer to the parsonage, we noticed the Minister's housekeeper at the door.

"Which is Mrs. Mickey?"

I stood still, as if paralyzed for a second, then I cleared my throat, "I am."

"A long distance call for you."

"A long distance call? What's the matter?" I'd never had no long distance calls before. I didn't even know what she was talking about.

"Come this way," I followed her into the parsonage, "someone is calling you from St. Louis by telephone."

"Three hundred miles…. And I can talk over it?" I flew to the telephone, and picked up the receiver. Static crackled over the wire. Then Henry's voice! I couldn't believe my ears. Something must have happened to Momma!

"Is that you, Georgie?"

"Yes," my heart was in my mouth. Dear God not my Momma! "What's the matter?"

"You've got to come home at once! I'm not going to have you running all over the country. You're married, and your place's at home!" Henry sounded so desperate, or had he started drinking, or was he just in one of his jealous rages.

Jealousy or not, the devil jumped in me big as a barrel. "My time isn't out! I have a contract. I can't leap right up and leave, because you say so! I banged the receiver down. Three hundred miles for that!

Upstairs in bed, thoughts of Henry annoyed me. I truly felt that he was a poor excuse for a man. Although, what was really bothering were my thoughts about lynching. I started to believe that lynching got burned into my brain, along with the sign, "NIGGER! DON'T LET THE SUN GO DOWN ON YOU IN THIS TOWN!"

My restless thoughts settled on the times - life as a black entertainer was not easy. In the South, we were still being shot at as well as lynched. Lodging on the road was often impossible. The next step for "The Alabama Jubilee Singers" was right across the state line in Arkansas. A terribly prejudiced place, where anything might happen. Racist feelings were running high, all down through that part of the country. Wherever we went, we were likely to meet the colored hate attitude. I knew the next time, it would be all too real. That made up my mind for me.

The next morning after breakfast, I expressed Henry's feelings to John. "My husband won't let me travel with you any longer."

"Does this have something to do with the "Nigger" sign blazing downtown Monette?" John stared at the dirty plates on the table, the crumpled napkins, the sordidness, the disorder, as if he were looking at the racial mess of America.

"Well…not exactly, but the hate signs did have a small role in my decision," I said, preparing to leave the table. "I wish the "Alabama Jubilee Singers" the best."

The Jubilee Company went one way, and I the other. I wasn't totally regretful. I'd had enough traipsing for a short time.

Chapter 18

When I got to St. Louis, Momma was sure glad to see me, and even Henry seemed happy. Yet, before I could unpin my hat, and place it on the dressing-case with my purse and gloves, Henry started his 'what a wife-ought to' type of nagging. "You're gonna stay home and not go running around the country!"

Henry's statement was so incredible. I didn't answer him right away. Finally, I managed to say, "Henry" as I gave him a quick once over - the lazy bum. "So long as you see fit to lay off the job, whenever you please. I'll go wherever I see a chance to make money."

Things went back just like they had been before I'd gone away. Soon I was singing at teas again, and in the choir - sitting next to Henry in the same old place. After a few weeks of this, I grew bored, and tired of the same old thing. I was just plain restless. I felt as if I were a caged blue bird, who wanted to sing and soar to great heights. Or I would surly burst.

New York began to sound like an elegant place to sing. I thought and pondered, about how to get there, for a couple of days. I heard Ernest Hogan and Matty Wilkes, one of the country's biggest colored attractions, were playing in St. Louis. They were boarding at my friend Alice's home. There were no black hotels where they could stay. The racial hatred was so horrible across America, that the more successful colored minstrel companies purchased their own train cars. This way they could provide the performers with a place to sleep.

Quick as a flash, I dressed in my best go-to-meeting pink shirtwaist and skirt. I rushed over to Alice's place. She eagerly ushered me into her warm kitchen. "Ernest and Matty are really here," she said smiling, as she twirled around. "I'm so happy, they chose to stay with me."

"I am, too," I hugged Alice, "and I'm so glad you invited me over."

"How's Henry these days?" Alice inquired, as she prepared a special blend of coffee.

"Same as ever - shiftless." I glanced over at the kitchen windows. The Autumn sunlight streamed through the ruffled yellow curtains. Little potted green plants decorated the sills. "Alice, your home is so beautiful... so warm."

"Thank you, but we need to talk about you." Alice set two steaming cups of coffee on the table. "Well?" she prodded.

"I just have to get away from Henry...." My voice trailed off. I knew it was my job as a wife to make my marriage work, but I was miserable."

Alice's large brown eyes filled with compassion. "How you going to do it?"

"Well, I thought if you'd introduce me, and I'd ask him to hear me sing." Just then Ernest Hogan and his wife, Matty, came in, but went right upstairs.

Alice wrapped her arms around me for a second, then a smile edged her mouth. "You wait till after dinner, Georgie. Now I know you never had a doubt about me introducing you," she teased. "We're friends forever...but most of all, I believe in you, Georgie."

Alice placed a warm cup of fresh coffee in my hand. I stood for a second, just breathing in the wonderful aroma, before I went out on the porch. Between sips of the blended Caribbean coffee, I hoped, prayed, and was sick, wishing Mr. Hogan would only take time to hear me sing. Once that happened, I was sure he'd help me get to New York.

Ernest Hogan and Alice finally came out after about an hour. He looked very jolly, and was dressed in a light gray suit, which made his dark chocolate skin look even darker. As my eyes glance quickly down his extremely manly body, I noticed he was wearing black patent leather shoes with spats. My eyes dashed up his body again. I noticed he had a diamond horseshoe in his tie. The big diamond ring on his finger, made me think back to George Walker. I got a warm feeling, thinking about how George Walker wanted me in his show. I felt more hopeful. God, Mr. Hogan was sure good-looking! He just had to hear me sing!

"Ernest, I want you to meet Georgie Mickey," Alice took a sip of the punch she had made, especially for her guests, before she continued, "we all think she has the most wonderful voice we've ever heard in a female. She's anxious to get to New York, so I told her I'd introduce her to you." She looked at me, and smiled, "Perhaps, you can help her."

I noticed Ernest Hogan's glance of approval about the way I was dressed, while I stood praying. "All right, Georgie. Can you sing for me now? I have a little while."

"Sure can," I replied, cheerfully, "if someone will play for me." I knew someone would, because the house was full of musicians, and teachers. Sam Peterson volunteered, and we got the "Holy City" chart out - which everyone had, it being very popular. Everybody in the house gathered in the living room, and on the porch, but I wasn't a bit nervous. This was my big chance, and I was going to make good!

"Please, play it in five flats."

"You would have to sing in a different key from the sheet music," Sam's long fingers moved gracefully over the keys, as he played the opening measures. You couldn't even hear a carriage going by in the street, or a tree shushing, or even a bird sound, it was just that quiet.

"Last night I lay sleeping...." Nobody was in the room with me for all I knew. Nobody was anywhere, and it didn't matter. The only thing that really mattered was the singing in me. "Hosanna! Forever more!"

For a moment more, there was absolutely nobody any place - just quietness, and then, "Georgie, I've never heard a voice like that in my life!" exclaimed Ernest Hogan, standing up, and clapping with great enthusiasm. I was so overjoyed. I forgot to say thanks. "You should be in New York," he continued, "but don't you worry. I've something in mind for you. I won't forget you."

I was overwhelmed by Ernest Hogan's praise. I didn't even know Matty Wilkes had entered the room. "You've got a great future," she said warmly. Then she smiled like all the sweetness in the world. Miz. Wilkes was dressed up all in white, and half way up her dress, from the bottom, were sprays of red roses. She wore red slippers, a huge red picture hat, and carried a tremendous shiny red leather pocketbook. The great big diamond rings on her fingers, flashed along with an elegant diamond brooch clasped on her bosom. Miz. Wilkes was so flashy. My mouth stood opened in awe. Then my heart started pounding with joy. The most beautiful colored woman on stage told me I had a bright future!

Ernest Hogan and Matty Wilkes rushed off to the theatre, while everyone crowded around me. "We never heard you sing that way, Georgie," Alice said, kissing me on both cheeks. "You were something transfigured."

"Well, Alice, maybe... just maybe, I'll get somewhere. Thanks!" I rushed home, and told Henry and Momma. Momma sat in her reading chair, and cried for happiness. Henry had nothing to say.

Chapter 19

Weeks went by and nothing happened. I went about wondering, would I ever hear anything from Ernest Hogan and Matty Wilkes? Fall faded... winter came...spring arrived, but nothing happened. Henry was most pleased. "So you thought you were going to New York, and be a big singer."

I had plenty of teas to sing at, but that made me angry. I felt I was wasting time in St. Louis. I knew if I didn't get out now - - I'd never get away.

Preparing to get dinner one May afternoon, I heard, "Mail for Mickey." I went down stairs - not much caring. Who was going to write to me? The mailman handed me a large strange looking envelope. I looked at the postmark - New York! Eagerly, I tore it open. A big sheet of white paper fell out! I grabbed it, and immediately looked at the signature - Ernest Hogan!

"According to my promise, I am writing to you. I am going to head a show, "Rufus Rastus," in the Fall, and would like very much to have you along. Rehearsals in August."

"Momma! Momma!" I raced up the stairs, "Momma, I'm gonna be in a show! In New York! Rehearsals in August! Gosh!"

Momma stopped ironing, and read the letter. "Oh, Tutti! Just like you always wanted! I'm so glad for you! What are you going to do?"

"Do? I'm going."

Henry raised the roof, and started speaking with more and more heat. "You can't go, less I go!"

"He's right, Georgette," Momma said shaking her head. "It isn't good for you to go off to a big city like New York less you have some man long. You never know what's gonna happen in those places!"

I immediately wrote Mr. Hogan, asking him to please use Henry in the chorus, as he had a very nice baritone voice. That I couldn't come if he didn't. Then I raised the roof with Henry.

In two weeks another letter came offering thirty-five dollars for the both of us. "Now, Henry, you're going, too. But if anything happens to you, it's on your head. I'm not going to come home."

We told everybody about the big show with Ernest Hogan

in New York! All of our friends gave socials. I got handkerchiefs, blouses, and all sorts of things. I didn't buy any new clothes, because we didn't have too much money.

The church people at St. Paul's said I was going to the devil. That those type of shows were sinful. They didn't want me to leave. I was their chief attraction - having recently put on a bazaar, and raised seven hundred dollars. Dr. Roberts settled everything. "You all shouldn't feel this way about Georgie. You aren't paying her anything." Then he put his arm around me, and tried to sound as neutral as possible, "and now she has a better chance to help support her mother. She's using her God given singing talent. Don't be selfish."

Eight o'clock, one bright sunshiny morning in the last week of July, I woke up with a smile. I put on my best pink shirtwaist and skirt, my straw sailor hat, and we departed for the train station. Momma, though delighted for me, wouldn't come to see me and Henry off. She just sat home crying. She'd had me with her all my life. Now she felt she was losing me.

We were in the seventh heaven of happiness - Henry more than me. He acted like it was he who was responsible for the whole thing.

The choir was all at the station. They brought a great big lunch, along with many boxes of candy. Everyone looked so dignified, standing on the platform, in their bright coloured Sunday best with gloves. We all shook hands. I kissed the girls goodbye. Then me and Henry got on the train right away. We didn't want it to leave without us. By and by, it started to move.

"Goodbye! Goodbye!" I wasn't even thinking about my friends, or Henry, or anybody, or anything, but New York! New York! The gypsy had said I was going to travell! And I was! I sure was!

PART 11

NEW YORK

Chapter 1
(1905 - 1907)

The train steamed into the Hoboken Baltimore and Ohio Station, on a beautiful August evening. We stood at the door peering out. This was New York? Well, we were sure disappointed. From what could be seen from the train, the station was a dreary, poor-looking place - nothing near as fine as St. Louis. It even seemed a lot smaller! The train came to a stop. We jumped onto the old worn platform, and looked around. There were even fewer people in New York than in St. Louis.

"Carry your bag, Madam?" A porter appeared at my side.

"Thank you. How can we get to "Hammerstein's Roof?""

The porter looked at us in an amazed manner - like where did these country cousins come from. "Cross the ferry to New York," he said over his shoulder, as he ambled off to help some other people with their bags.

I brightened. "Then this isn't New York!"

Henry sighed happily, "What a relief!"

But the porter said 'the ferry'… "What's the ferry?" I asked the porter, as he passed us carrying some bags.

He frowned, as if we were bothering him, "The boat that carries you cross the river to New York. He pointed to a boat that looked like our excursion boats back home. We were so anxious to get to "Hammerstein's," we weren't bothering how we got there. We quickly grabbed our suitcases, rushed into the ferry, walked through it, and went outside. What tall buildings across the river! That was for sure New York! We didn't have tall buildings like that in St. Louis. We couldn't count the windows, reflecting the setting sun. All sorts of lights and signs winked like lightening bugs.

In the midst of everything, amberish lights spelled out "Hotel Netherlands!" I'd never even dreamed of so many lights, signs, and buildings! This was New York…the city of hope, the city of dreams, the city where the buildings across the river sparkled like diamonds. The sparkling lights were all my prayers and hopes, reaching up into heaven to God, Himself. Before we realized what was happening, the boat was in New York.

I was so intent on getting to Ernest Hogan. I paid nothing no mind. I just went straight to the nearest porter. "How do we get to Hammerstein's Roof?"

"You can go by street car or take a cab."

A cab sounded speediest. "We'd better take a cab, Henry. We're strangers here."

"Better be careful with the money, Georgie," Henry warned, with a worried look on his face. "We only have twelve dollars."

"Oh... I can't wait, Henry! A cab will take us right to the door fast! Anyway, I can get money from Mister Hogan."

Many low-built open carriages were standing right there. Even though they all had white drivers, we went up to one, and just got in....

"Hammerstein's Roof!" We moved slowly out among what seemed like hundreds of other vehicles, all trying to go different ways with the utmost speed.

It was beginning to get dark, but we hardly noticed. So many lights! More lights than we'd ever seen in our whole lives! The hurry! The rush! It spellbound us.

"You're strangers, aren't you?" The cab driver asked after a few blocks.

"Yes, sir!" I answered as I watched the cityscape slide by - the exciting awareness of New York thrilled me.

"Well, you're now on Broadway." The cab driver proudly announced.

Broadway! For the first time in my life, I couldn't say a thing - only look. What beautiful shops! Such lovely things in them! The windows were lighted, too, and magnificently decorated. St. Louis's shop windows were never lighted at night, and as far as decorations! - we only had them at church socials and Christmas!

"That's," the driver continued, "the Flatiron Building."

"Why 's it called that?"

"Because it has three points - just like a flat-iron." I thought about Granny and Momma ironing with that heavy flat-iron. Then suddenly a big sign: "HAMMERSTEIN'S VICTORIA ROOF GARDEN!" My heart jump in my throat. I couldn't take my eyes off that sign, until we got to Forty-second Street.

In front of the theatre the lights were even more blinding. A large sign announced, "THE MEMPHIS STUDENTS WITH

ERNEST HOGAN, THE UNBLEACHED AMERICAN!" Who paid the driver, I don't know. But the next thing a splendiferous uniformed man barred the way.

"Where do you think you're going?" He demanded in a gruff voice.

"To see Mr. Hogan," I said with all the confidence I could muster.

"Go to the stage entrance." He pointed the way. We flew around to that door.

"Where do you think you're going?" This time it was an ordinary-dressed individual - old, too.

"I just got in from St. Louis! I want to see Mr. Hogan," I pleaded but the old doorman seemed unmoved. "Believe me...I'm going to join his new show!"

The old man looked at a sheet of paper on a clipboard, then looked up at me. "You'll have to wait. He's on the stage, and the act's just gone on."

Loud bright sounds of quick music, and laughing jumped out from beyond the doorman. We stood as far inside the door, as we could, and looked right out on the stage. My eyes and ears glued themselves to the colored men out there. They wore different loud-coloured plantation suits, and regular kind of yellow plantation hats. They were playing all sorts of string instruments including banjoes, guitars, mandolins, and everything! In the center of the stage, one of the most beautiful colored women sang.

"Who's that singing?"

"Oh, honey," the old man smiled, "everybody knows that's Miss Abbie Mitchell."

Her voice was glorious. She was singing "Swanee River" even better, it seemed to me, than Black Patti. Gosh! That was ages ago that I heard Black Patti...now I was on Broadway in New York City. Abbie Mitchell finished singing, but the audience tore the house down, and made her sing "Swanee River" over and again. Then she sung something else, bowed gracefully, stepped back, and sat down with the rest of the company. They all seemed to sit on the stage like minstrels.

The band struck up, "Go Way Back and Sit Down." Then Ernest Hogan came out on the stage. Thunderous applause! He sang, "Go Way Back and Sit Down," which was most popular that summer. Although, it was when he sang "If Peter'd Been A Colored Man" that the audience went wild!

The Memphis Students played something fast. Two girls jumped onto the stage. They danced like mad. Hogan beat a tambourine on his head, elbows, hands, knees, feet - just everywhere! The act finished in such a whirl of excitement. I never dreamed that it was possible - the entertainers and the audience where hilarious with joy - such applause! Then Ernest Hogan and the Memphis Students bowed, waved their hands, threw kisses over and over, before they rushed off on the other side of the stage. I stood completely bewitched.

People from the act walked passed us and went outside. Men pulled the scenery up, and set things out on the stage. What was all that for? Then a voice said, "Goodnight, Mr. Hogan." I turned toward the sound. Ernest Hogan was being swallowed up by the crowd, waiting to catch a glimpse of him. He stepped into an open carriage. I tore out, flew up to it, and put my hand on the horse's bridle.

"It's me, Mr. Hogan!" I yelled, "Georgie Mickey! I just got here from St. Louis! Remember me?"

"I sure do." He smiled, the million-dollar smile he was noted for, as his diamonds gleamed in the night-lights. I was so enthralled at his even talking to me; I just grinned all over!

"I'm Mr. Henry Mickey." I'd forgotten any such person, but there he was pushing right at my side - ready to get his share of glory being passed out.

"Please to know you. Come on you two, jump in. I'm just going to eat." Eat? Minute I heard that it dawned on me, no food had passed my lips since early in the day. "Yes…of course." The next thing I was riding besides Ernest Hogan. Henry was sitting in the little front seat with the valises.

"We'll go to Jack Nail's to eat," Mr. Hogan exclaimed, "it's one of my favorites." That sounded scrumptious. My career had started right in on the good foot.

Jack Nail's was a small restaurant on Sixth Avenue somewhere between Twenty-Eighth and Twenty-Ninth Streets. It seemed colored performers went there to eat. I was so high from all of this new excitement. It was as if I was floating on a cloud…but I sure ate!

Mr. Hogan finished eating, and patted his mouth with his napkin - his diamonds glittering. "Where you planning to stay?"

I patted my mouth with my napkin, just like Mr. Hogan did. "We don't know."

"I'll call up Shep Edmunds. He's the man who writes my songs. Maybe," Mr. Hogan drank some port, "just maybe, he can put you up." He drained his glass, "I'll be back in a minute," he walked towards some people in the back.

I looked around the tiny little restaurant. The place was packed with nothing, but colored people laughing, talking, and eating away. They seemed to be so happy. They all looked so fine. Most of the men wore big checkered suits, spats, and large diamonds. The women had on bright coloured dresses, with diamonds in their ears, and all over their fingers. Some even looked liked they had red colour on their faces!

Ernest Hogan returned to the dining room, paid for our meals, then we walked towards the door. "It's all fixed. You go right over, and they'll take care of you. Meet me tomorrow afternoon at one o'clock. Shep'll tell you where."

Shep Edmunds lived in a white-plastered three story house. When we rang the bell, a young woman came to the door. "We're looking for Shep Edmunds. We're the people Mr. Hogan phoned about...."

"Come right on in!" We followed her up two flights of practically dark stairs. "Here's the room Mr. Edmunds has for you." Then she turned and just walked away.

I went into the room first. Henry put his feet in, and that was about all he did put in. There wasn't enough space for both of us. There wasn't any light except through a window in the ceiling. Although, there was a tiny thing I knew was a gas jet. I'd never had gas before. I wasn't crazy about it now. Coal-oil lamps back home gave more light than that scary, little, white-blue flame. It smelled bad, too.

None of this, however, mattered much. I was completely dazzled with the glamour of seeing Mr. Hogan, and New York. I simply fell on the bed exhausted. Finally, Henry got into the room. Two people couldn't be in the room, unless one was in bed. That sure was funny. Everything in this city was so funny. I fell fast asleep.

It was just getting light the next morning, when I opened my eyes, crawled over Henry, and got out of bed. I dressed in my pink shirt-waist, skirt, and sailor hat. I went into the hall so Henry could get out of bed.

We wandered off looking for a place to eat. We had the worst meal of ham and eggs, we'd ever tasted. So far eating and sleeping in New York, was much worse than anything we had back home. But I still didn't care. This was New York.

Nine o'clock in the morning, found us meandering up Fifth Avenue. In 1905 Fifth Avenue was the millionaire residential section of New York. I'd heard and read about the splendid mansions that were supposed to line this brilliant avenue. Yet, we walked and walked, until we were tired, and didn't see anything special - only lots of nice brownstone houses. Some houses were of white stone, which was a bit more like we expected.

We reached a green place with trees. We found out this was the beginning of Central Park. I was very happy to find the trees, and some benches where we could sit down.

"This is a pretty park, Henry, but not nicer than Forest Park at home."

Henry scratched his head, "I wonder where all those millionaire's mansions are? Most of the houses don't look better or any different than St. Louis?"

A white man sitting nearby said, "If it will help...that house over there is the Gould's...that's the Rockefeller's...the Astor's, and that house belongs to the Vanderbilt's."

I turned looking towards the homes. "If millionaires live in those places, they should be more showy to let the world know about it. Fifth Avenue isn't even laid out with shrubbery. The houses haven't any grounds at all. Back home everybody has grounds and trees. Here, I haven't seen any trees outside this park." I was so disappointed. I just stopped looking for the millionaires' homes. Instead, I thought of Mr. Hogan...what rehearsals and being a great singer in a big show would be like. The next thing I knew, it was time to go to rehearsal.

When we got to Mr. Hogan's, he was pacing up and down. "I've been waiting for you! I've called up a lot of people to hear you sing!" A man was busy at the piano. "This is Fess, my musical director. Now you come with me." We walked over to a wall phone, where Mr. Hogan quickly dialed a number. There was a pause. Then he said, "She's right here, the only female baritone in America! What? Sure! Georgie, I want you to sing "Holy City" to this man over the phone. Fess'll play for you."

Over the phone? Well, singing was singing. It didn't matter how, and where I did it. Hadn't I even spoke to Henry over the phone, when he was three hundred miles away. "Five flats, Mr. Fess, please." His fingers danced across the ivory piano keys.

I stood before the mouthpiece, and sang as though thousands were listening.

The last deepest tone, and I was finished. Mr. Hogan grabbed the receiver. "What do you think of that? Didn't I tell you! I'm bringing her right over!" He jumped up and down. "Mr. Hurtig wants to see you at once! He's the man who's backing the new show!" I thought I was going right through the roof! Mr. Hogan yelled, "Come on, Henry!" We tumbled down the stairs, and off we galloped in a hansom cab.

"Mr. Hurtig has a partner, Harry Seaman," Mr. Hogan continued, while Henry and me watched the sights of New York slide by, "Jules Hurtig and Harry Seaman are white men who produce colored shows. They produced "In Dahomey" with Williams and Walker."

"Yes, I know," I beamed proudly. "Mr. Walker wanted me to go with them."

"I'm sure glad you didn't." Mr. Hogan smiled, then laughed out loud. I could barely contain myself, because of the throbbing excitement in the cab.

We went into a building, and walked up two short flights of stairs. Then entered a room where white girls sat pushing their fingers down on little machines - typewriting! My did they sure favour Mr. Hogan. He said, "Wait a minute, Georgie," and went into another room. A big picture of the "In Dahomey" company hung on the wall. That's exactly where my picture was going to hang, too.

"Come on in…this is Mr. Hurtig, and this is Mr. Seaman." Their office represented nothing but success. It was like a song and dance of fame and money.

Mr. Hurtig looked at me for a moment, then smiled, "You have a wonderful and most extraordinary voice. You will be a sensation in the show." I was bursting with joy, listening to this real distinguished looking handsome man say such nice things about my singing.

Mr. Seaman was most amiable, too. He eagerly joined Mr. Hurtig in complimenting me. "…And we are glad to get you."

By this time I was grinning all over. I drew up my shoulders, and felt so big! "Thanks. I hoped you'd be pleased…Williams and Walker wanted me, but Momma wouldn't let me go. I wasn't finished with school."

"That's good," Mr. Hurtig roared with laughter, "thank

goodness for Momma. We'll see you Monday morning at rehearsal."

Mr. Hogan put his arm around me, and we happily rushed out of the building. I was so excited that I couldn't even see where we were going. Nor had I given any thought about Henry. I knew he was part of the backdrop. "Rehearsal's at Odd Fellow Hall," Mr. Hogan said as we walked towards a cab, "this is wonderful... the show and all. Shep'll show you where it is. Nine o'clock sharp. Monday morning. Now let's celebrate!" Ernest Hogan carried us all over town. I sang for all sorts of people. At last we landed at Marshall's Restaurant, uptown on Fifty-third Street.

Marshall's Restaurant, in 1905, was the place where white and colored people both met. "Most of the Memphis Students live over this place," said Mr. Hogan, very much the sophisticated older man. "There's no place like this...believe me...in the world!"

The restaurant itself was just two big rooms filled with plain tables and chairs, but overflowing with people. All sorts of bejeweled celebrities, who's names were always in the newspapers or on sign-boards, were there in the flesh! Eva Tanguay, the reigning comedienne, a shining blond, elegantly dressed, sat leaning across a table, talking to a short colored man. That astonished me. I'd never seen colored and white people being so social.

"Who's that colored man?" I squeezed Mr. Hogan's hand, as the excitement bubbled within me.

"Don't you know?" His face broke open in a broad smile, "That's Dan Avery of Avery and Hart - the famous comedians."

"Ah...yes," I fought to keep my joy under control. As I continued to look around the room, I noticed lots of colored men and white women sitting together... some sort of intimate. Then I kept hearing the name Hannah Elias. She was the most talked about person there. "Who's Hannah Elias?"

"She's the colored woman that the white Senator just married," Mr. Hogan explained. "He bought a big brownstone house on Fifth Avenue." Then he casually added, "with Japanese servants...she sure is living high."

People kept shouting to Ernest Hogan, "Hello, Uncle Rube," and he'd shout back, laugh, and carry on. There was all this talking, too, of a Mr. Harry Thaw who'd killed a Mr. Sanford White - some great architect given to throwing tremendous parties.

He got his entertainers from Marshall's.

A man with a large hooknose chuckled, "Remember the San Juan Hill riot, Uncle Rube?"

"What's San Juan?" I was so curious about everything. "What happened there?"

"Well, San Juan," Mr. Hogan smiled broadly, "is between West Fifty-Ninth and West Sixty-Second Streets, and is mostly lived in by Irish and colored people. Where the Irish live is called Leprechaun Hill, and the colored part is San Juan Hill. One night I was coming home from work, got near my corner, when I heard all this fighting and yelling, between white people and colored people. I ran into a grocery store, where they new me. But some whites spied me, and came after me. I took a handful of money, flung it into the crowd. They immediately fell on one another, trying to get the money," he roared with laughter, "then I got out the back way."

So New York was really like St. Louis after all. That story had sounded like Kerry Patch and the Micks. Although, the white women and colored men were sitting close together here, which made it very hard to believe that whites and colored tried to kill one another in New York City.

Even after being in Marshall's for a little while, I was still amazed. Everybody was eating, drinking, smoking, and talking at such a rate. Some drank some almost clear stuff called champagne - very expensive and highly desirable. The women all had on gorgeous dresses that were shining with glittering stones and diamonds...some with soft veils and lace dresses. I felt most small in the company of all this grandeur.

Finally we spotted a corner table. It was the only one left. We moved quickly towards it, before someone else got it. The three piece band played sweet music. Ernest Hogan gave me a menu, "Order what you want." Wow! There was plenty to order... and the prices! I saw - Club Sandwich. That was a rarity I'd heard of before, and never eaten. I ordered one promptly.

At the next table, a man sat drinking out of a tall mug. That was something new, too. "What's that man drinking out of the mug?"

Mr. Hogan seemed to enjoy teaching me. "That mug's a stein, and cold beer's in it."

Beer! I didn't drink no liquor! "Lemonade, please." I didn't want nobody to think that I was a loose woman.

The band stopped playing. There was a roll on the drums.

Everything and everybody grew quiet. A man stepped to the middle of the room. "You all know Uncle Rube is getting ready to go into a new show, and his people are arriving daily. Tonight we are most fortunate in having with us an outstanding singer from the West. I am told this little lady, has a voice that's never been heard before in New York!" Well. Who was this rival? "Uncle Rube - our own Ernest Hogan - has brought with him, to - night - Miss Georgie Mickey!"

Everybody clapped, and Mr. Hogan said, "Georgie, I want you to sing for these people."

"Is it all right to sing "Holy City?"

"Sure." With a lot of pride, he led me to the piano.

All those celebrated eyes looked at me. "Five flats, please." I opened my mouth, and sang like I was possessed. After I finished, everybody crowded around me. "What a find! Where did you get her, Uncle Rube?" Ernest Hogan just stood, and flashed his million-dollar smile. "I brought her out of the wild and wooly West!"

George Walker and his wife squeezed through the crowd. "We regret so much it wasn't our luck to bring you out, and help make you the sensation you will surly be."

I smiled, thanking them, while Mr. Hogan held my arm very possessively. Then we went back to our table, but people still kept coming up congratulating me. I thought - I'm not dressed fine as all of you, but I've got something to offer, too.

I was so full of joy that I introduced Henry to everybody. He stuck his chest out, and acted like he was the cause of it all. He was obviously thinking - Well, she's my wife. She belongs to me.

Chapter 2

Nine o'clock Monday morning found Henry and me in Odd Fellow's Hall. It was a long dingy place with benches, chairs, and all sorts of people - from everywhere sitting and standing around. Some were singers who had been brought from different choirs - same as me. Then some were dancers from places far into the deep South. They all looked animated and hopeful. Although, some people had been in shows before. They all looked as though nothing unusual was going on. Everybody was sort of casual.

"Where ya'll from?" A blubbery but pretty girl drawled, sweetly.

"St. Louis...." Then the rest of them at the table asked our names, and we all got to talking.

Ernest Hogan wasn't there, nor Hurtig and Seaman. A tall brown-skinned man with silvery hair went around getting names and addresses.

"Who's he?" I asked a gorgeous dancer with a fawnlike neck.

"Oh, that's Mister Green who directed The Smart Set." She peered into a small mirror, as she arranged her hair. "Mr. Hogan brought him here to direct this show."

After taking several more names, Mister Green came over to where we were sitting. "I'm pleased to have you with us. Mr. Hogan has told me all about you, and your wonderful voice."

"Thanks..." Footsteps and laughing came up the stairs, interrupting me. Everybody got their party manners on, and smiled a whole lot, as though trying to look pretty.

Hurtig and Seaman came in with Ernest Hogan. Mr. Hogan flashed his million-dollar smile at all of us, before they sat down talking. I could feel the power of success coming from the three of them. Since everyone was new to the show, they all perked up, and seriously took notice.

Then Mister Green called the singers one by one. The majority were marvelous singers, but not one voice as low as mine. I ran up and down the scale. Everyone applauded. "We've never heard such a range in a female voice!"

"All right everybody, you're dismissed. Be back here nine o'clock tomorrow morning." Mister Green yelled as he checked his schedule.

So that's all rehearsal was about. Well, it hadn't even been as hard as choir practice at home. Yet, it was very different, because of the new accents, and the wonderful strange voices. Henry and me sauntered along Broadway looking for an inexpensive restaurant.

He was so delighted with everything. "You know, Georgie, my voice was one of the best there." I shrugged, and gave him a quick smile. Henry was really something else. His voice had almost been the weakest. Well, he was probably thinking they'd keep him to keep me.

When we got back to our tiny room, a note was pinned to the door. "Please, come over to my place. Ernest Hogan." We rushed right over there like bats out of hell.

"I want to try you in some of the special numbers," Mr. Hogan said, with his million dollar smile. He sat listening to every note, and every facial expression the Sextette made. Henry wasn't in it.

The next day Mister Green started the chorus singing in parts. This was more like choir rehearsal back home. The only difference was the music was peppy, and so many more voices carried the parts. It was harder, too, because most of the singers learned by ear. A few of them could actually read music. It was such a pleasure, however, singing and being paid for it. The people were so open and expressive with their talents. I was happier than I'd ever been!

"Five o'clock! Everybody dismissed! Georgie Mickey and other Sextette members report to Mr. Hogan's house tonight. Eight o'clock sharp!" Mister Green announced, reading from his scheduled notes.

"What about Henry?"

He looked down at his pad, "…Oh, we won't need him."

Henry glumly followed me downstairs. "I don't understand why I can't go?"

When we finished rehearsing that night, Ernest Hogan asked me to supper with Mister Green. The minute we walked outside to get a cab, Henry was standing there waiting for me. "Where you going, Georgie?"

"To Marshall's with Mr. Hogan and Mr. Green."

"You're going home with me!" Henry demanded, his face distorted with anger.

I cringed... not a scene... Dear God, not here in New York. "Will you please excuse me, Mr. Hogan and Mr. Green? Henry is waiting for me."

A stunned silence held all of us for a moment. Then Mr. Hogan's million-dollar smile broke across his face. "Oh, bring him along. Come on, Henry."

"No," Henry stated flatly without a smile, "we're going home." Then he grabbed my arm and ushered me down the street. "You didn't tell me you was going to any supper! You were trying to slip off. You didn't come to New York to run around with any and everybody! I don't know those men!"

I jerked my arm from Henry's grip, "You look here, I don't intend to be worried by your jealous outbreaks. You're not going to interfere with my work! I came here to make a career, and nothing you can say or do will stop me!"

We quarreled all night, almost evolving into violence.

Chapter 3

At rehearsal the next day, everybody was making-up-to-me and friendly. They were crowding around, calling me "Honey!", and "Georgie Child!", and such stuff. I didn't understand it until the beautiful dancer, with the fawnlike neck, asked, "Have you seen The Clipper, Miss Mickey?"

"What's The Clipper?"

"Biggest theatrical paper in town!" She exclaimed, her big brown eyes grew as wide as silver dollars. "It's so exciting!"

"Oh...that's the place Mr. Hogan took me to sing the other day. What's in the paper?"

"All about Hogan bringing you from St. Louis, and how wonderful your voice is!" That made me feel topnotch!

When we knocked off for lunch, there stood Mrs. Macon waiting next to the door. She was a woman we'd known very well back home. But we hadn't seen her for five years, since she'd moved away. Her husband got a job as chef on the Gould's private railroad car. "Mrs. Macon! I'm so glad to see you! How did you ever know to come here?"

"I read in The Clipper that you were rehearsing here." She enclosed me in a sweet fragrance, as she hugged me close. It sure was swell to see someone from St. Louis.

"Where's Henry?"

"Inside...." My voice trailed off. I looked down.

"How do you ever get along with him out here," Mrs. Macon said, her voice thoughtful and remembering, "I mean...with his trifling and jealousy?"

"I'm not getting along." I fought to control the anger, and frustration running through me. "He's worrying me terribly." I decided to look her directly in the eyes, so that she could really understand my pain. "Every step, Mrs. Macon... every time I move...Henry's at my heel! Also, my living condition aren't good. The room we have is so small one of us has to stay in bed until the other is dressed!"

"God almighty," said the plump and motherly, Mrs. Macon. "You sure have your misery. You come up to dinner. I'm sure I have a room, you'll like. I'll be tickled to have you."

"Oh, Mrs. Macon, I certainly am grateful!" I kissed her,

then smiled, and walked towards the rehearsal room, with one long over-the-shoulder glance at dear sweet Mrs. Macon. "We'll be up after rehearsal!"

The next day we moved to Mrs. Macon's - 171 West 63rd Street. That was quite a way uptown. But our new room was large, and had two big bay windows overlooking a lovely garden laid off with flowers and benches!

Only one thing puzzled me. Washed clothes were hanging out in the back yards to dry, without anything to keep them up so high. "How do those clothes stay up?"

"You really mean you don't know?"

I smiled as I stared at the bright colourful clothes. "No, I really don't know."

Mrs. Macon laughed, like she was hearing the funniest joke in the world.

"What's so funny?"

"You, Georgie." Then she explained how pullies worked. Just the same I sat, and marveled how clothes hung mid-air in New York! I even wrote to Momma, but she couldn't grasp the idea either.

Chapter 4

The beginning of the third week, our twelve dollars gave out. How we'd managed on twelve dollars for two weeks is now a mystery to me. But the third week, I knew I had to send Momma some money. So I asked Mr. Hogan, and he gave us a week's salary - thirty-five dollars. I kept half for room rent, and to live on.

Lots of times, we could have saved money, through men in the show, wanting to take me to lunch. But Henry always made such a disturbance, I wouldn't ever go. He was by far the most jealous man, I had ever met in my entire life. Anything could set him off on a raging tirade.

The rest of the show began to arrive - mostly leading players from other shows. Kendall Troy, a colored tenor, national sensation and a very handsome man, arrived looking like God's gift to every female. He was most sought after by white women. Then came Anna Cook, an extremely dark, ugly, fat soprano, but could she sing! As black as Anna Cook was, her husband was completely opposite. He was so light; he looked like a white boy.

Chic, the little brown skinned dancer and singer, I'd met when William and Walker were in St. Louis, arrived. She was wonderfully talented, and real nice-looking with such large green eyes. She was supposed to be the sweetheart of one of the leading men, and everybody knew her. Having made a reputation, as a great performer, she carried herself as if she were better than most. Some people didn't like that.

She'd supposedly been with this particular leading man in two shows. Everybody said she was madly in love with him - had even left her husband for him! He treated her lovely, when he was in good humour. Yet he had very little time for her, because (like most colored men in his group) he was very sought after by white women. Aside from his apartment on San Juan Hill, he had a room at Marshall's, where these women were always coming. Most of the colored men of his set had apartments there paid for by these women.

Chic remembered me from St. Louis, so we went back and forth to rehearsals together, and got very chummy. Having been in the profession a long time, she was able to show me things, I didn't know - like makeup.

Before I came to New York, I never put powder or anything on my face. Everyone knew only extremely low females, boat hussies and such, were the only ones who painted their faces. Although, once when I went to Chic's room I was flabbergasted!

There she sat before a glass, which had two gas jets on each side. All sorts of jars, tubes, and boxes stood on a table in front of her, and horror of horrors - she was putting black stuff on her eyes! It came from a little black pan, she held over the gas, and she put it on her very long eyelashes with a toothpick! - a upward motion for the upper lashes - a downward motion for the lower! The black stuff looked like little pills when she got it on.

"What are you doing that for?"

Chic peered into the mirror. "To make my eyes look larger, of course."

"I'll never use it," I shook my head, "no… I have very few eyelashes. I'd burn my eyeballs sure."

She, also, had a little round box - " Warneseon"s Rouge for the Face." That definitely was the very height of wickedness, but she rubbed it on light and cheerful with a rabbit's foot. I stood like I was glued, watching her paint her already lovely face into a masterpiece. She put paint on her lips, too. Now she was even more beautiful than ever! All of a sudden, she jumped up without any warning, and said, "Excuse me. I must go down the hall for a minute."

Promptly I sat down, and looked into the mirror. Gosh, I was sure plain. It suddenly occurred to me that my looks were just ordinary. Perhaps…just perhaps, makeup would make me more glamorous…more glittering…more show business looking.

I saw a can - "Stein's Theatrical Powder, No.2" - kind of brownish looking stuff. I put it all over the front of my face, making certain not to touch my neck, or under my chin. I looked dreadfully white! Rouge might fix it. I put on a lot. Not so good. With all this rouge, powder, and no eyelashes, I looked like a clown! I was brown all over excepting my face, and that was a most peculiar colour!

Chic came back in, took one look, and whooped with laughter - almost cracking her side. "You're supposed to make up your neck and shoulders, too." That crushed me, but I did look funny. "Always come to me before you go on, and I'll see how your makeup is. I'll always show you."

"Thanks…." I felt I'd found some one really interested in

helping me get ahead.

    We came and went together, and I was extremely happy with her. Henry was usually at general rehearsal. Chic and I had special rehearsals for the Sextette, and her numbers. Mr. Hogan had put me in all of her special numbers, too. Now I truly felt like I had a friend. I was happy with my new life in New York, and with show business.

Chapter 5

Six weeks after we started rehearsing, Mr. Green decided the show was ready to open. The Company was all called together for a dress rehearsal. For two and a half hours we sang, danced, and took the whole show down. Then suddenly Jules Hurtig rose up, "This show isn't ready to go out! Tomorrow morning we will start rehearsing again!" We had just finished rehearsing from nine in the morning until we couldn't no more. This was every day for six weeks - without pay! Well, this was show business, and I loved it!

The next morning began weeding out. Henry was the first to go. He had an all out hell raising tantrum!

"I'll go, but I'm not going to leave you here!" His eyes narrowed dangerously, "It's not my voice they don't like...it's being your husband! They want you for themselves! You're coming home with me!

"I told you in the beginning, if anything happened, I wasn't going home! I'm not! You have no job. We have no home of our own to go back to." I stood straight with my hands on my hips, and glared at Henry for a second, "I'm going to stay where I am!"

"Nah," argued Henry, "I won't leave you out here to turn into a whore! I know those stage men - not one decent one! You'll come home, or I'll kill you!"

"It's no use fighting." My voice grew calm because I was just plain weary of it all. "Listen, we haven't any money. So why don't you leave me on here to make some money, while you go on home and get settled? By that time, I'll have a lot of money saved, and I'll come home, too."

He thought on that a long time. "Well," he finally broke the silence. "I don't have much of a choice, do I? Anyway, I guess that's not such a bad idea...."

Quick, fast, and in a hurry, I got some money from Mr. Hogan, bought Henry's ticket, and saw him off the next evening. I was never so glad to get rid of anybody in my life.

The next morning after a Sextette number, one of the lead men asked, "Henry gone?"

"Sure is."

"That's fine," he licked his thick lips, "now, maybe I can be his understudy."

"What do you mean?" I eyed him suspiciously.

He smiled slyly, "Oh, you'll find out." He adjusted his bulging crotch, then took his place stage left.

I didn't ask him anything else, nor did I give it another thought. I was much too happy, and too busy to care. Besides Granny had spoken to me a long time ago about certain things...sex was like swimming in the creek. The creek was so delightful to look at, so refreshing to swim in, but never bathe in it, unless it was safe - people did drown sometimes when the creek was rough and dangerous. So I had no plan to swim with any of the leading men.

We went on rehearsing day and night for three weeks. Three days before opening in Troy, New York, they gave me "Old Kentucky Home" to sing with a male quartette. That caused a lot of jealousy, but it didn't bother me any. I'd come to New York to make a career, and a lot of fame and money. I intended to do it or bust!

That very same night, I was handed a telegram. It was something I'd never received before. But I knew usually they meant unhappiness. It must be about Momma! I ripped it open. "If you want see husband alive come immediately. Dr. Roberts." Dr. Roberts was the pastor of St. Paul's Church - at home! The whole world tumbled over me. I didn't know what to do. Something sure must be wrong are Dr. Roberts wouldn't have sent me a telegram! I rushed to Uncle Rube.

He read the message. Then he looked at me, his face conveying an amused contempt. "Georgie, you're very foolish to go. It's only Henry trying to get you home," Uncle Rube sighed deeply, as his face crinkled with disgust, "but if you go and find nothing wrong with him," he forced one of his million dollar smiles, "you come right back to your job. Meet us in Troy!"

I was on the next train for St. Louis, with all kind of imaginations racing through my head. - Would Henry be dead? If he wasn't dead, what would happen to my career? If he was dead, would they blame me? At last the slow moving train lurched forward into Union Station, and my heart lurched with it. I couldn't wait. I called Dr. Roberts, immediately. "This is Georgie Mickey! I came home soon as I could get here! How's Henry?"

"He was at church Sunday morning. What are you doing here? Are you tired of your new world so soon? The church will be so pleased to have you back."

"Wait a minute. Please…listen to this telegram." I read it to him.

"My dear child, I never sent you a telegram, but Henry did say last Sunday that you'd be home soon. Don't worry," he said, trying to quiet my fears, "nothing was wrong with him then. He looked just fine."

Looked fine! I'd show him! Soon, I was running up our stairs two at a time. "Momma! Momma!"

Momma came running out of the house with panic written on her face. "Tutti! What's the matter? Why did you come home?"

"Where's that Henry?"

"He's not here," she caught her breath, "he said he was going out to look for work. …Well, you look good, baby."

"I'm okay, Momma…it's just Henry. That's a lie about work. Henry and work have long since parted friendship." I poured myself some hot coffee, "He and me fought all the time in New York. He was forever so jealous. Then three days before I was opening, he sent me a telegram saying he'd kill himself, if I didn't come back. I thought it was from Dr. Roberts. That's whose name was on it."

"I sure am amazed," Momma shook her head, as she sat in her chair rocking. "Not a thing wrong with him."

Just then my so-called dear husband walked in, "Georgie!" He came towards me.

"Don't you come a step nearer. I hate a liar. If you think I'm staying, start thinking different." I went right down the steps, wired for my fare to Troy, and came back to Momma's.

"I'm leaving tomorrow."

"If you do, I'll kill you!" That was a lot of bushwhack. During the time Henry had been home, he'd written threatening me, and everybody in the show. In case he did turn up though, I'd bought a small revolver, which was in my dressing case. I had purposely sat the case nearby, on the other side of the room. I wasn't afraid of no Mr. Henry Mickey.

The next morning when the express man came for my things, Henry jumped into the middle of the room. "If you leave this house, it will be over my dead body!" The baggage man reached for my trunk. "Put that down!" Henry yelled at the top of his lungs. "Get out of here!" The man started without the truck. I pulled my gun out, and pointed it at Henry, Momma screamed, then cried, and broke down in her chair. I wasn't paying her no mind. I wanted to win, and winning was being a part of Mr. Hogan's show in Troy.

"You just said if I leave, it will be over your dead body." My eyes locked fiercely into Henry's, as I spat out my words in precise deadly tones. "Well, if you don't let the man move my baggage, I will not try to kill you, but you certainly are going to hurt!"

Henry was so stunned, he just slumped down on the sofa, and burst into tears. That was the end. I wasn't going to have no sympathy for any man that stood in my way of success…especially, a weakling like Henry!

Momma and me got to the train, just in time to hear the conductor yell, "All aboard!" I kissed Momma, jumped on the step - Little Tutti hitching train rides to school! The little girl who loved music! …before her memory began she had a passion for music - and the train chugged out of Union Station. All I could see was Momma waving, and crying on the platform. I was very upset. Then I realized, I only had one more day to get to Troy and opening night!

Chapter 6

Around eight o'clock in the morning, I got into Troy - having hardly slept and dead tired. Even though the sun was shining brightly, all I noticed was what a sorry-looking town Troy seemed to be. Then without any help, I dragged myself into the theatre. Such confusion. Such running. I went straight from the stage door, onto the stage, and into rehearsing the opening chorus - a hotel scene in which I play a chambermaid. I didn't even have time to think about being tired. In fact, the tiredness left me, as I went through the female quartette, the Sextette, two or three chorus numbers, my own specialty with the male quartette - and was I happy. This was my right place. This is where I belonged.

Rehearsal kept up... lighting... scenery hanging and shifting, seventy people, and a multitude of scenes to dress. The costumes were lovely, especially the Minstrel costumes. They were green with little red flowers. With them we wore red shoes, red stockings, and large red picture hats. The end men and girls were dressed in red, white, and blue tights. In my "Kentucky Home" number, I wore a gingham dress, low-heeled shoes, and a large red, white, pink bandana. The boys were in overalls. We only stopped rehearsing, when it got close to curtain time. Although, at eight-fifteen we were full of energy, primped up, and ready to go!

Finally, it was show time! "Overture! Overture!" People rushed all over, laughing high-nervous-like. Then all at once, everything went dead silent. Everyone lined up facing the curtain. A dull murmur could be heard from beyond the curtain. The cast was breathing hard with energy. Then the music started, we got to beating time, and before we knew it the curtain rose up.

The show went down like clock-work. Each number went bigger than the other. We brought the audience to its feet with "Kentucky Home." Encore after encore. When we supported Henry Gregg in the ballad, "Consolation," the audience couldn't be held. It was a personal triumph for me because I... Miss Georgie Mickey, the female baritone, got the raves.

We played Syracuse, and started out on a tour of one-night stands that lasted six weeks. During this time we never got any rest. We'd open in a place with a matinee, a night show would follow, after which we immediately left for the station. Then we would stretch out on hard benches, waiting two or three cold hours for our train to carry us to the next town. Most of the time, we'd arrive just in time, to get from an hour or maybe two hours of sleep, before the matinees. Also, between shows we'd try to snatch a few hours of sleep in our tiny dressing rooms - getting enough sleep was somewhat of a problem, but it was show business. We loved every minute.

Sometimes there wasn't even any dressing rooms. We had to dress in halls, and passage-ways. Even when there were dressing rooms, most of them were practically useless - having no running water, just small broken bowls and pitchers for washing. Most places didn't even have a looking-glass. We made up in our own hand-glasses propped on a rickety table. If we could find a table.

In several towns the footlights were just gas jets. One theatre used only coal-oil lamps for house and stage lighting. The stages were usually made of rough, unplanned boards, which made dancing almost impossible. A lot of the dancers came off with bleeding feet from splinters, brushing through their thin shoes.

Most of the theatres were so old, we could see chucks of sky through their roofs. That was very unpleasant when it snowed and rained. One time it rained so hard on the stage - it was like a small flood. We couldn't put on the minstrel scene.

During this tour, I first became truly acquainted, with stage superstitions and etiquette. Whistling in the dressing room was a definite sign someone would lose his job - usually the one nearest the door. To bring peanuts in the theatre, or put hats on a bed was unforgivable. Yellow was a colour of an evil omen. That was why our first dress rehearsal had gone bad. The chorus had worn yellow shoes. It was after we got rid of those, and got the red shoes (an extremely fine colour) that we had such success. Rabbit's feet and bad dress rehearsals were the best of luck.

Colored female singers and dancers became prominent in the growing business of entertainment. Talent played a major role in pushing performers into the limelight. But it was a woman's physical shape and the image she projected that influenced producers and managers. The men who hired women singers and dancers, who wrote the parts, wanted women to play sweet young things. Or play a romantic interest of some well-built man, a sexual tease, or the butt of a joke. Colored critics felt that light-skinned mulattos succeeded more often, than dark-skinned women. So even in the entertainment world, women were still expected to act the way men envisioned them.

Stars of shows were just that - stars. That wasn't a superstition. It was a fact. A chorus girl was just another piece of furniture in the picture. Understudies were the same as pieces of poison ivy. A lot of the stars said if someone stood in the wings, trying to learn something, they were wishing them bad luck. The stars never mixed with lesser members of the company, and were jealous of their stardom.

Salaries ranged from chorus - eight dollars a week to fifteen. When an entertainer made twenty-five, he or she was a top-notcher. Principals got from thirty-five dollars to fifty a week. The highest anybody ever got was Abbie Mitchell, seventy-five dollars a week, which was really going some - real big time! The star of the show, of course, received more than that - maybe one hundred or one hundred twenty-five! I got eighteen a week, and transportation. Expenses weren't paid by the management. Transportation meant only the train-fare, not sleeping accommodations. Only a few of us ever had berths. We couldn't pay for them. So we sat up, and slept in our clothes night after night.

However, starting with Chicago, we would start traveling the "circuit," often playing a split week; three days in one city, a day to travel, and three days in the next city. We all sighed with relief, at the thought of getting away from the one nighters.

We performed every day, even Sunday, which seemed to be the biggest day of the week out West. After knocking around like this in tank towns for six weeks, we finally arrived in Chicago. It was a Sunday morning, and we were to play the "Great Northern." We were booked to start with a matinee that very Sunday afternoon.

The theatre was situated in the same building as the Hotel Great Northern. I was so tired when we got in the lobby. I didn't stop to think of price or anything. I vaguely remember someone saying matinee, while I got a room, and fell into bed.

The bed was something. Such a treat… a luxury to actually stretch out in a honest-to-goodness real bed… the solitude… peace…

When I woke up, I instantly rang the bell. "Bring my breakfast, please, in a hurry. I have a rehearsal and a matinee."

"A matinee… today?"

I stretched and yawned lazily. "Sure."

"It's an extra one then. This house has only Sunday, Wednesday, and Saturday matinees."

A quick shudder went through me. "Well, this is Sunday."

"It is not. It's Monday."

"Monday!" I threw my clothes on, and raced downstairs. Everybody seemed to be rehearsing my parts. The moment they saw me they yelled, "Where have you been?" I told them. "That's some story. You expect us to swallow that?" Finally, Uncle Rube went up to the hotel with me, and everything was settled. But I sure got out of that hotel fast. I just couldn't wallow in elegance, and be a star.

Chapter 7

After Henry had gone to St. Louis, men were always asking me to live with them, but I refused. Nothing was on my mind, but my career. I wasn't interested in no loving. Now almost everyday, except for Chic, there was jealousy in the company about my success. She was my best friend - always helping me. When I was in trouble or lending me money. She would cheer me up, when I got downhearted about Momma or Henry. But most of all, she taught me lots of valuable things, like how to wear costumes, makeup, and such indispensable stuff. I was with her most of the time.

One night we all went to a party, except for Chic. Everybody was drinking very heavily. I never drank anything, but lemonade. However, this lemonade sure had a strange, strong taste to it. First thing I knew my head was twisting off my shoulders. I felt dizzy, peculiar.... "I better go home." I stumbled towards the door in a drunken stupor. It was hot. A strange girl said, "don't you feel well, Georgie?"

I stared at all the unfamiliar faces in the room, then shook my head. "No... I wanna go home...." I felt very faint, and there was a persistent pain tearing at my gut.

"You can't go alone. I'll go with you." It didn't make no difference who went, so long as I got out of there, and home.

As we descended down the stairs into the chilly night air, I felt worse and weaker by the moment. I don't even remember how I got home. But the next thing I knew, I was in bed all undressed, and this girl was kissing me violently.

"Hey!" I pushed her away from me. "What's the matter with you? What are you doing?"

"Aw, don't kid me," she said shrewdly. "You know what it's all about."

Know what it's about? I got most sober. I remembered all those stories about Chic, and myself being "Lady-Lovers." So this was what they had meant - this laying in bed all undressed, being pawed and kissed by another woman.

The girl cuddled next to me again, with her lips half parted. "God damn you! Get out of this house at once! Go tell your friends, what they sent you to find out, is a damn lie!" She instantly grabbed her things, and shot out of there like Lucifer, himself, was chasing her. I ran my fingers across my lips, and smelled the awful combination of stale liquor, and the dead fish stench of that girl. Then I got violently sick, and finally fell asleep.

The next day I overheard, "All this talk about Georgie Mickey and Chic is nonsense. We sent somebody to try Georgie out, and she 'most killed the poor girl!"

After all of the insanity that happened last night, I was puzzled. Could two people, of the same sex, mean anything to one another emotionally? The girl had tried tactics, I would only expect from a male. I didn't like it. The only thing to do was ask Chic about it. After all, she had been just about everywhere. She would definitely know.

Assuming a light-hearted mask, I got to the theatre extra early that evening. I left word with the stage manager, that I wanted to see Chic. Right after she arrived, we went up on the stage, and sat on the steps of "Posturing and Strolling" opening scene. Chic felt such delicate matters were best discussed in an artistic atmosphere.

The stage just had a dim work light. The theatre stretched out all spooky and waiting... I could hardly see Chic's face. I proceeded to tell her all about the night before. "What's this, anyhow? What's the meaning of it?"

"Well...you've got to know sometimes...you might as well know now," said Chic, gazing out at the empty seats in the theatre. "When I was in England, and English woman did the same thing to me. I discovered two women can mean as much to each other, as two people of the opposite sex. Mostly women who feel that way, just can't help it.... It's right to them. They're not very happy - many of them, but they have to go on. Some men are like that, too."

All of this didn't quite sink into my understanding. I was grateful to know what it was truly about.... I still liked Chic more than anyone. But it was still quite a surprise, and without a doubt most puzzling.

Chapter 8

While I was still in Chicago, Henry suddenly appeared with his same "me husband - you wife" tricks. We had the usual quarrel. I paid the usual debts, and made the same promises to go home. Again he departed threatening to kill me, if I didn't obey him. After this God awful boring quarrel, I happily left with the Company for Kansas City.

We stopped in Peoria to put on a diner car. Everybody was so lighthearted, because business had been so good in Chicago. It looked like "Rufus Rastas" was going to make money wherever it played. That meant another season of work.

A waiter came through, "Lunch! Lunch!" That sure was a familiar voice. I looked up. There was the man who had stood up with me, and George when we got married.

"Red, imagine seeing you here!"

"Where you on your way to Georgie Mickey? Home?"

"Not yet. We're going to Kansas City."

"You sure is traveling," he pressed his hand into mine, "come on have lunch with me, and tell me all bout it."

With an eager smile I said, "Sure. Thanks." I immediately rose from my seat. As I followed Red towards the diner, I realized I'd forgotten how nice-looking he was, with his light brown skin and nappy red hair.

When I emerged from the diner, Uncle Rube was pacing through the coach, like he was a caged beast. "Georgie Mickey, I won't have any member of my company cutting up with a common waiter in a white coat! Exactly, what in the world is going on?"

"Ask me no questions, Mr. Hogan, and I'll tell you know lies - " I looked at the disgusting expression of superiority on his face, before trying to walk pass him. He grabbed me by the arm.

"Now, I won't have it, Georgie!" Uncle Rube shook with rage. "You best remember that!"

The train was still in the Peoria Station. So I went to my seat, took my bags, and went home to St. Louis. I was filled with misery, and anger - both at Hogan and myself. It later turned into humiliation. I truly wanted to go back, but I had too much pride.

Although, while I was home, it actually felt good not to have the pressure of constant strangers. This gave me a chance to really think. It was basic. I loved show business with all my being. It was everything... it was my life... my world. Henry was pleased with having me home. But I was beyond thrilled when a telegram came almost as soon as I arrived. It begged me to return to the show at once. I race to Louisville.

Louisville was as lovely as when I first started my traveling career there. It was with Bishop Waters of the African Methodist Episcopal Zion Church... seemed like centuries ago. I got a chance to visit with a lot of old church friends. I was extremely happy. Being back with the Company, singing, and dancing, made me feel like I had been stitched together again. Then we departed for St. Louis! The excitement of playing in my own hometown was thrilling. Also, whether Henry would shoot me was enough to keep me thoroughly perked up, and alert.

Chapter 9

St. Louis! In spite of fears, it was a swell feeling. I was going to sing for friends, again - people who'd known me since I was a brat. I went straight home where Momma was waiting. She looked fine, but very upset.

"Henry got your letter and was most angry," she sighed deeply. Then as an afterthought she said, "Do sit down, baby... at least you look well."

"Thank you," I dropped down onto the sofa. I was really tired of conversations about Henry, with Henry, or anything to do with Henry. They seem like such a waste of time. I smoothed my hair back, and straightened the collar on my blouse, while I waited for Momma to continue.

"He said you wrote you didn't intend to live with him no more, and you would be pleased if he left this house."

"Momma, I feel like I'm dying of thirst by the side of a fountain. I just don't want Henry. He keeps trying to block me, from getting to the fountain of show business. I need to water my creative being."

"But Georgie," Momma said, studying me tranquilly with her deep brown eyes, which saw far and much too much. "You married him. Why don't you give him another chance?"

"For what?" I rapped my fingers on the polished surface of the end table. "He won't work, so I have to make our living. If you insist I'll stop singing, but I do want to make money for you."

Momma never mentioned Henry and me again.

We went to church, which was crowded with everyone I'd ever known, including Mr. Henry Mickey in his usual choir place. I didn't feel any affection looking at him. I just had a bad taste, and loathing. Right before the service finished, Momma and me left. I didn't want no "who-stuck-John" from Henry.

We had Sunday dinner at the organist's house. I had just bit into a mushroom stuffed with crab, when the doorbell rang. I cringed - it had only been an half an hour, since we'd seen Henry. Then the well-known voice started screaming at the top of his lungs, "I want to see my wife! I know she's here!" Momma and me looked at our delicious untouched meals, and sighed. We cut out through the back door. That jealousy scene of Henry's ended any thought of my going to parties or socials, while I was in St. Louis.

After that every time I stepped on the stage to do a number, I didn't know whether I'd get off alive. Henry had said he was going to kill me. Night after night, I was an easy target, singing away with a smile, and dancing feet. Immediately after I finished with the show, I'd dodge through the main entrance of the theatre, instead of the stage door. Then I would rush home in a cab. The last night of the show, friends had told Momma that Henry had said he was definitely coming to the theatre to kill me - so I didn't work.

While the show was going on, I kissed Momma goodbye, slipped through the backyard to Union Station, found the sleeper car on the train, and hid in my berth. The train left directly after the performance. I was sure happy to hear those wheels moving! Although, I had no idea - in my wildest imagination, that it would be nearly seventeen amazing years, before I would lay eyes on Momma again!

Chapter 10

Pittsburgh, Cleveland, Cincinnati, and then we were on our way to open at the "American Theatre" - a new fifteen cents movie house on Forty-Second Street, New York! New York! - that's the goal, the moment I had been looking forward to all my life. After seeing Black Patti perform in St. Louis, I used to spend hours daydreaming, on our front porch, about the glitter of performing in New York City - traveling off to exotic places to perform - but it was truly just about the joy of New York. I knew after being successful there, nothing else much would ever top it!

Opening night was more excitement than I'd ever known before. Reports came back stage that the house was filled to capacity with whites and colored. There was a hum of thrilling electric conversation floating in the air...giddy talking... the happy laughter beyond the curtain. The audience had all heard of the show's success on the road. They were eager to watch us strut our stuff. I stood silently next to my dressing table for a moment, sucking the wonderful energy in... it was truly a special treat to be performing in New York.

Then the overture started, everybody whispered "Good Luck! Don't be nervous!", like it was the very first time we'd ever played. The stage manager whispered, "Quiet!", and the curtain rose with a roar of applause.

Every number was a triumph. The whole company was in the quick, and happy spirit of success. They danced and sang in complete joie de vivre. The quartette supporting Greg Olson, gave encore after encore for their Daedalus number. And "Kentucky Home" - my specialty - brought the house down. The next day the papers raved, and "Rufus Rastas" was a smash hit!

We played to capacity audiences throughout Manhattan in various theatres - "Hurtig's and Seaman's," "The Yorkville," "The Grand Opera House" (still standing at Twenty-Third Street and Eighth Avenue), and closed for the summer having trouped thirty-five weeks. Now I was a real professional singer, who had been with a big hit show, for one of the best managements in town. Besides I was a full grown up woman, twenty-two years old, who had quite a knowledge - or so I thought.

Chapter 11

While touring after we left St. Louis, the three girls and me, who formed the quartet supporting Herbie Thompson, seemed to do well as an individual feature. We decided to rehearse together. Maybe, get some Sunday concert engagements. That was what Sunday vaudeville shows were called then.

It was after we had closed "Rufus Rastus" that I finally realized that I hadn't saved any money. I'd sent every penny to Momma, except for my own expenses. Thank goodness the other girls took me in. We all felt we should stick together, and rehearse every minute we could. We'd be ready just in case we got lucky, and an opportunity arose.

All of the camaraderie made me extremely happy, but underneath I was rather discontented. Abbie Mitchell had the most glorious voice in "Rufus Rastus." She was still studying music with Sembrich. Everybody said my voice was wonderful, but I knew it wasn't as polished as her's. I wanted my voice to be absolutely peerless, but I never had any money to take the lessons. Voice lessons became my chief ambition.

After a couple of months, Ernest Hogan put on a vaudeville set called, "The Minstrel Mokes," and we all had big fun working in it. Although, the act played all summer at Hammerstein's, the quartette still went right on rehearsing.

Then one afternoon Uncle Rube stopped by, and watched us rehearse our entire act, "You girls are really sizzling. How would you like to start doing some Sunday concerts?"

We couldn't believe our good fortune. We stood there not saying a word, with surprised expressions on our faces, finally I said, "Yes...yes, we sure would."

Uncle Rube rehearsed us a few days, named us "Creole Belles, and formed us into a nursemaid act with baby carriages and dolls. We opened at Hurtig and Seaman's 125th Street House with gleams of happiness shining through our eager eyes.

To our delight we were put on stage right before Virginia Earle. She was one of the highest paid singing sensations in the United States. We went over so big, she refused to follow us. Our future seemed to be made. We were engaged every Sunday. We sang in vaudeville houses, beer gardens, and at parties. Yet, I still never had enough money for singing lessons.

By the last of August, the second season of "Rufus Rastus" started. "The Creole Belles" was being spoken of everywhere, and all the agents, and managers wanted us. Although, we were offered more money by "Black Patti," "William and Walker," Cole and Johnson's "Red Moon," and "The Smart Set," we didn't want to leave Uncle Rube, and "Rufus Rastus." He'd been our benefactor, and we weren't going to let him down.

Chapter 12

"Rufus Rastus" opened in Boston. The only thing I remembered about that city, was a girl I'd known back home. She married, and moved here from St. Louis. It was September - cold, dreary, drizzling night. Boston was the bleakest place I'd ever seen. I poked through the icy streets, until I found the house, where my friend lived. I rang the bell. After what seemed like ages, the droopiest woman shoved her head out. She told me my friend had moved months before. Weariness and despair settled on me.

Not knowing where to go, I wandered for hours, lugging my heavy bag. My hands and arms felt like icicles. I just couldn't find any place to go that I could afford, or who wanted me. As soon as I said I belonged to a show, they would slam the door in my face. It finally sunk in that to be in the theatre was the worse possible thing in the world. Actresses it seemed were supposed to be floosies. After awhile the rain got so bitter cold, and the bag so heavy, that I decided to go back to the theatre. Maybe, they would let me sleep there. I was just plain filled up with hopelessness and misery.

Suddenly, as I turned the corner, I was face-to-face bang with Chic! "Where you going, Georgie?" She asked as she studied my weather beaten face.

"Oh. I'm so unhappy. My friend from home moved, and I can't find a place to sleep. I'm going to the theatre. Maybe, they'll let me stay there."

"Why didn't you tell me that you needed a place to stay earlier?"

I looked down at the snow, "well, I just thought…anyway, I just didn't want to bother you."

"Don't be silly," she laughed, "and you don't have to sleep in the theatre tonight. There's a room where I am. It's on the third floor. There's no fire in it, but the landlady might be able to put in a little stove."

Immediately, everything got extremely bright. The little room was most cheerless and cold, but I was happy to have it. The landlady didn't have any little stove. So we went to Chic's room. It was a first floor back parlour with a hot grate-fire - very elegant to sit before.

"Well, what's going to happen this year with "Rufus Rastus?" I wrapped my hands around the warm mug filled with hot apple cider. "Will there be as much excitement as last year?"

"Don't know about the excitement, Georgie, but I hope I won't have as much unpleasantness." Chic laughed bitterly, as she stared into the fire. Then she quickly said, "His Highness, has been on a rampage with his white woman, nearly ever since we got back from last season. I hardly ever see him, but I can't do nothing about that. Anyway, now we're out on the road again, he'll be lonesome. He'll have to be coming along to me pretty soon."

I listened politely while Chic went on and on about her love. Although, all I could think of was how, this very man, had repeatedly made advances to me, and everyone else in the show. He sure was a skunk.

The rain and wind were fierce, but we were so cozy with the fire, and the sad talking... By and by, I went upstairs.

My room was freezing! I hastened into bed, tried to sleep, but it was so cold it was impossible. It got so icy I couldn't stand it. I hopped out of bed, went downstairs, and crawled into bed with Chic. She didn't say anything... so warm... soon... I was fast asleep...

Suddenly, a doorbell was ringing violently! A loud deep voice... in the front hall. Our door banged open!

"Come on! Get up!" Bill, Chic's boyfriend, yelled. "You're going with me!" He shook her hard with one hand, while he continued drinking from a bottle with the other.

"It's so cold. I don't feel like getting up, now..." she complained, but she sounded so pleased that he'd come for her.

"It's warmer over my place." He emptied the liquor bottle, with one long drink, then yelled, "damn it! I said get out of bed! I'll sit in the parlour, till you get your clothes on, but hurry up!" He went into the parlour. We could hear him walking around, switching on lamps. Finally, we heard a chair creak, and we knew he had settled himself to wait for a few minutes.

"I told you he'd be after me. He's lonesome. He's got nobody else. Now he's falling back on me, just like always." There was such a pleasure in her voice, such a quickness as she flung her clothes on, and flew out to him!

The door slammed loudly. All of a sudden, I felt like the whole earth, sky, and everything had come down on me. All things stopped - ceased to go around. Such emptiness was in me.

Why should she have to go to a man, who would throw her over tonight, if he found somebody new? Even if he didn't, he'd probably beat her before the night was over. He usually did. I truly just didn't understand that sort of love.

I couldn't get to sleep. The wind, and rain were so loud, and wailing, and lost… the fire was dead…everything was all black, cold, and lonely. It all wondered in my head - over and over - why did I feel like I'd lost something precious? Why did I feel sick to my stomach? It didn't make sense. I couldn't figure out why, I was just laying there, staring out into the darkness, unable to sleep. The wind and rain went crying, and moaning on. A tree scraped up against the house, and everything was forever unhappy. I had such a lump in my throat. I ached all over. I was completely miserable, as I listened to the bells from a nearby church, sang faintly on the early morning air. I looked out the window - the sky was starting to lighten, and I still could not sleep… and I still felt a lost.

Chapter 13

We played New York, and subsequently Detroit, but "Rufus Rastus" didn't go over so strong after that - Abbie Mitchell, our internationally famous prima donna, left to open the Pekin Theatre in Chicago. It was the first theatre managed and run by colored people. Bob Motts was its head. Such stars as Miller and Lyle, Clarence Muse (one of the biggest movie people), John Larkins, and Shelton Brooks (composer of "Some Of These Days), came out of it.

To take away from losing Abbie, Uncle Rube thought of something to pep up business. Everyone besides doing their own stuff, would play an instrument, and sing "Mandy Lou." Furthermore, he decided, we should all be thorough, so he bought cello books, for us who played that instrument. Soon he had us all taking cello lessons. He had an extreme thing or some kind of crazy bug about it.

"Georgie, if you learn that cello properly, and with your voice - you'll be the biggest sensation out!"

I made no effort to respond as Uncle Rube continued to express his opinions, about the glory of the cello. All I knew was, that the big fiddle was, a pain between my legs. I hated it. So one sweet day, I departed to Mr. Hogan's bathroom. I deposited my darling stringed tribulation, and never saw it again. That was the end of my sensational career as an instrumentalist.

Chapter 14

For three days we were scheduled to play Wheeling, West Virginia. The theatre there was so antique, that the audience boxes stood right flush on the stage. During the very first performance, Chic's slipper flew off into one of those boxes. Accidents like that happened all the time. We didn't even think on it. Although Bill, her boyfriend, was madder than a bloodthirsty shark circling a helpless cripple victim.

"You threw your slipper off to get those white men to pay you some attention!" He glared at Chic, as if to murder her with his eyes. "I'll teach you to meddle with other men! You're going right back to New York! I'm going to get you fired!"

There was a deadly silence. For a second, we just all stood there staring at each other. Then Chic covered her face with her hands, as tears streamed down her cheeks.

"But listen, it was an accident. We all saw it. Anyway, she's sick," I pleaded, "her lungs are bad!"

"I don't give a damn!" Bill's face hardened into a mask of stone. Then he turned, and disappeared back stage.

Well, it sure enough sounded like he had his eye on some one new. So with a heavy heart, I took Chic to the train. She cried and carried on, but there was absolutely nothing more she could do. Bill could have people hired and fired whenever he wanted to do it.

When I got back to the sparsely finished room that Chic and me shared. I felt so alone. Yet, I didn't especially want anybody around. Then it began to dawn on me, nobody was anywhere near I could even talk to, or relate my feelings of tremendous lost to…it was just plain scary. I was absolutely without a single person. In about seven days, I knew fully what a friend she had truly been. I'd spent practically all my time with her. She'd always been around, when I wanted her. The complete lack of close friendship, came over me for the first time in my life.

Day after day, I went to a room, which was always in a different town, but always the same - forsaken and forgotten. The boarding house rooms were eternally similar in smallness, dinginess, and misery. I'd sit brooding and lost. Without Chic, the bloom was definitely off the rose. Finally, I couldn't stand it anymore. I went to Bill.

"Why don't you, please, let Chic come back? You're really all wrong about her, and she's in New York with no work, no money, and sick!"

"You're asking me favors. That's rich. I've asked you to be with me many times, and you always refused. Now, you want me to do something for you," his voice became thick with sleazy lust, "well, how about doing something for me first?" I cracked him in the jaw, and flew out of his dressing room.

My songs were taken away from me. My quartet was taken out completely. The Company began saying, "Well, Georgie Mickey's gonna come down off her high horse now. She's not so big!" I couldn't quit the show. We were too far from New York. Plus, the season was too far-gone for me to get any other engagement. Anyway, if I didn't have a job, Momma would have to go back to hard work. She hadn't had to do any of that, since I could make a living. I couldn't even bear to think of it!

Then right after a matinee, a week later, Bill called me. I went feeling sicker than when he'd packed Chic off.

"Georgie, I've decided, since the quartet, and your solo is out," he paused for a moment, his face growing into the same immovable stone mask. Then he continued, not even looking at me, but at his well-manicured nails, "and you can't dance - we will have no further need of you. You're going home when the week ends."

I was appalled by his continued cruelty. The most devastating thing was that I had nobody to advise me about what to do. My insides were ripping apart at just the thought of losing my career. I didn't know what to do. So I did absolutely nothing, but more sitting, more brooding, until it was time for me to go on stage.

The Saturday evening before my last performance, Bill called me again. "What have you made up your mind to do?" I couldn't answer him. I just cried. "Why don't you make up your mind to what I want?" He said levelly, moving to his dressing table, and searching through his jewelry box. "You can't make it by yourself, regardless what talent you have," he continued flatly. He found a gold ring, shoved it onto his finger, and snapped shut the jewelry box. Then his ice-cold black eyes bore into mine. "In this business, you got to have a friend to get on. You stay with me, and I'll not only send for Chic, but see you get a raise. Think it over...." I did. I signed the lease deal with my body.

I'd seen and heard things like this happened to other girls. That it was an old story in show business. You had to take it, or leave it. Now to get my own way, I would have to allow Bill to get his way. Every fiber of my being revolted against it. But my and Chic's being, in the show, was totally dependent on what Bill wanted. So Bill got what Bill wanted. The following week Chic returned.

I got the madness out of my head, by rehearsing the quartet for hours each day. Even though the pain had not gone away, the edge had been dulled by keeping myself very busy. When we didn't have matinees, I went to see other shows or vaudeville acts. I learned all I could about presentation methods, scenery, and costumes. I was determined the quartet, and me, were going to play in New York vaudeville houses. After that we would be ready to play anywhere.

Chapter 15

The season ended, my luggage with all of my clothes had been stolen - probably by some of Bill's people - but, "The Four Creole Belles" arrived in New York to find a vaudeville engagement at Keith's Fifth Avenue House. That one wonderful engagement, assured me, that we were really getting away from "Rufus Rastas". We were beginning to stand on our own legs. In fact, everything seemed to be changing, and for the better. Chic had decided to leave Bill. That was about the greatest news of all. She was still my best, and only friend. So anything for her good delighted me.

The Keith engagement was like a fantasy love affair that had finally come true... love that gave me warmth, when there was no heat, coming from anywhere else. I shivered with excitement. When you played a Keith House, you were supposed to be a top-notcher. The Fifth Avenue was second to the best vaudeville house in town - Hammerstein's Roof being generally thought the absolute best.

Vaudeville in 1907 was like present day English music hall entertainment. The show usually consisted of acrobats, comedians, dancing teams, animal acts, and singers. The favourites were Eddie Leonard, Eva Tanguay ("I Don't Care"), Elsie Janis, Williams and Walker, and Eddie Foy. Mr. B.F. Keith was at the head of the whole business.

The reaction to our act - especially Chic's dancing, and my rendition of "Love Me And The World Is Mine," which I was the first to sing - was so favorable, we were convinced we could take care of ourselves. We got in touch with an agent. He looked our act over, and booked us a date immediately. Ernest Hogan was madder than a toad. We had committed the ultimate sin! - we dared to get a job without his help! Anger had pierced every one of his nerve endings. He went into a total rage!

Hogan confiscated our baby carriages, costumes, and music! We had other music, but no orchestra could play it. We just plain needed our orchestrations. Although, one of the girls did play the piano. So we dashed over to where we were booked, and told the manager everything.

"Have you any dresses?"

"Yes."

"Wear those." The short chunky manager said, as he straightened a flashy gold ring on his stubby finger.

We did. We looked terrible. The dresses were all different styles, colours, and ages. Some were long. Some were short. One was up on one side. One was down on the other. We sure looked a mess, but we were showstoppers. We were a sight for sore eyes, but were we ever triumphant musically.

That was short-lived glorification. Hogan soon saw to it, being most influential, that we got no more work. Well, he wasn't going to stop me. I'd made up my mind to survive no matter what. Now I realized that we needed our orchestrations, more than anything else. So I went up to the place where Hogan lived. I knew the old woman who ran it. "Uncle Rube sent me for some music," I announced casually.

"Hep, yourself," she said, with snuff in her bottom lip. Then she slowly kept sweeping the parlour.

I quickly turned to head towards Hogan's room. "You know," she stop me in my tracks, "I just love the way you perform…you and those Creole Belles."

We exchanged smiles. "Well, thank you." I started for Hogan's room again.

"Well," she stopped me again, "I remember when colored folks first started on the stage," the old woman spit in her spittoon, and started ransacking her memory, "yea, it was back right after that big war, between the North and the South, when colored folks started forming their own groups like the Charles Hicks Georgia Minstrels, and Lew Johnson's Plantation Minstrel Company. But Lordy," she shook her gray nappy head, "they blackened their faces, and drew them red and white lines around their mouths - they was nothing fancy like you are today."

I laughed politely, "Yes, I never liked black face either. I always felt that they were making fools out of colored folks. Well, let me get this music," I forced another smile, but my insides were quivering. I was praying that I could get the music out of there, without Hogan walking in on me.

"I don't want to keep you from your work," she started sweeping the parlour again. "I know all of you young folks are in a hurry."

I took a deep breath to steady my nerves. Then into Hogan's room I went, got the music, took it home, and sat up all night copying the orchestrations. I picked up copying music from

Mr. Fess, Hogan's musical director. The next morning the music was back in its place. The Creole Belles had orchestrations. Now everything looked like it was going to be easier.

We figured wrong. Hogan blocked us at every turn. He told agents the quartet was disbanded. That was always a sure way of losing jobs for an enemy. Things got so bad, we didn't have any money. Just very small amounts, from entertaining in cheap beer gardens, and like places. All of my dreams of studying voice seemed to be fading. I didn't even have enough money to send to Momma. It got so awful that we didn't eat all the time. But we kept on rehearsing, and learning new songs.

We had been keeping all of the windows shut, against the unusually cold winter weather. A girl we knew, rushed into our small place, with good news. It was like all the windows had been flung opened, and the fresh air was like an exquisite luxury. "You're wanted at the Marinelli Office. You better go right over!" I raced downstairs. How to get there the fastest? The new subway? But I was afraid of it! Well, this time I'd have to risk it! H.B. Marinelli was the biggest foreign booking agent in New York! I tore into that office.

"Well, Georgie Harvey. What's become of the Creole Belles?"

"We're still together."

"That's strange," the handsome Mr. Marinelli frowned. "Our lookout caught you at Keith's, and he's been asking for you every since. Mr. Hogan tells him you've disbanded."

Although, I shuddered at the memory of Hogan's horrible backbiting, I maintained a look of confidence. "We have not. We've been rehearsing everyday."

"That's excellent." A pleased smile crossed his face, "how would you girls like to play Europe?"

"Europe!" It was here...at last! "Does a duck like to swim?"

"All right then. We will arrange for the quartet to sail in about two weeks. Don't say anything to anyone. Wait to hear from us."

I could hardly get out of that blessed office. I was so excited. I could hardly wait to tell the girls. I was floating on a cloud. Even the scary-looking subway didn't frighten me this time. I just plain wasn't aware of it, or anything, except my dream.

I rushed into the tiny apartment. "We're going to Europe!"

I took my heavy winter coat off, and flung it in the air. "Lord, have mercy, we're going to Europe!"

"Europe?" They all asked at once.

"Yep... in about two weeks... Mr. Marinelli told me, but you mustn't tell anyone else!"

Did we rehearse. Money or no money...food or no food, we were going to Europe! We were getting rid of Ernest Hogan, "Rufus Rastus," and anything that was bothering us. We were going travelling, and singing, and...it was just all so wonderful!

Then about two A.M. one morning, I was awakened by a wild ringing. The front doorbell. A big banging - at my door. "Who's there?"

"Telegram!"

"Telegram!" I threw my heavy coat over my nightgown, and rushed to the door. George Mickey was coming. Something had happened to Momma. I wouldn't be able to go to Europe. My hand shook from nerves, as I ripped the telegram open. "Creole Belles be ready sail within three days. Act fallen out. Want you replace." I thought I was going to pass out with joy.

"Girls, girls, wake up! We're going! We're going in three days! Europe! We're honest to goodness going, girls!" But they didn't make a sound. They couldn't. They were absolutely struck dumb. Then tears of happiness filled our eyes...we smiled at each other, as the past...horrible months of hunger, and abuse, and our bright future kept shifting and interlocking in our minds.

Nine O'clock the next morning found me at the H.B. Marinelli office. "You are to sail Saturday on the S.S. Princess Alice of the North Deutscher-Lloyd Line for Breman, Germany. Then you are going to Budapesth..." That meant the Danube River! I'd be able to see for myself whether it was really blue! Austria, Hungry, Germany - Europe was going to be a real place - not a coloured bunch of marks in a geography book!

"Well... it's all too lovely, Mr. Marinelli, but," I was determined to take the risk, "we have no money and no costumes to go anywhere."

"That's all right. It will all be taken care of when you get there. Your transportation, berth, and all, will be paid. Our Berlin representative, Leo Masse, will meet you with advance money. Mr. Marinelli took it all so matter of course.

I whirled home again. Only this time, I smiled to myself as I got on the subway train. This new means of transportation was getting to be an everyday conveyance now.

The moment I entered our apartment, I yelled, "It's definite! It's true! We're sailing Saturday!"

Julie drew in a deep breathe, and asked astonished, "Saturday?"

"You better believe it!" I walked around the room, with my hands stretched towards the ceiling, laughing.

"Oh, my God, today is Thursday!" Chic giggled, her big eyes sparkling.

"But what are we going to do for costumes?" Shirley Faye asked, with a sad smile playing on her lips.

"That's right, and how we gonna get there?" Lucy sighed, her large bosom heaving wearily. "I mean, we have no money."

"Sure enough, we have no money." The expressions on their faces were so funny. I could barely stop laughing. "You don't worry your heads about it. Everything's taken care of. I'm the one should worry. I have nothing to wear, since someone decided to steal all of my clothes. I have not a cent, but that's not going to stop me." Beaming from ear to ear, I walked over, and flung the closet door open. "Ladies notice…there's this one dress, and my one suit, but to Europe I'm going. Thank heavens it's warm and cozy… well, in my mind, so I don't need a coat!"

"That's well enough, but what bout my husband?" Lucy's forehead wrinkled up.

I flopped into the big easy chair, feeling smug and jubilant. "So, telegraph him right away, and ask him."

"What bout my husband?" Shirley Faye questioned, sitting on the side of the chair.

"Mmmm… let's take him along." I said serenely, feeling good about how our discipline had paid off with singing engagements in Europe. I paused for a moment, as their faces started to vibrate with happiness. They all took on lighter more carefree spirits. "Anyway, Shirley Faye, we'll need somebody to look after the baggage, don't we? Well, your husband can do that. Each one will give him so much for his salary, and he'll be a protection in foreign countries."

Just the words - "Foreign countries" - made it all sound so thrilling, mysterious, wonderful, dangerous. From the moment I first saw Sissieretta Jones as Black Patti, I started dreaming about traveling… so many dreams, as I placed little dots on maps…and the gypsy had told me. I had worked, and worked, and suffered my bit. Now it was going to come true. I relished every moment of my newfound happiness. Then I offered up a big prayer, thanking God.

Saturday morning found us at the Hoboken Ferry. The girls had big suitcases and trunks. I had only a paper bag with underwear, a nightgown, and my only dress. I had to even borrow my ferry fare. I was that broke.

What seemed like forever on the ferry...eternity, we finally got to the ship. "Tickets"

Chic opened her pocketbook. "They aren't here!"

I was stunned...shocked, almost in a state of agonizing grief...this couldn't be happening. "Where are they?"

"I must have left 'em home in the top drawer!" She answered slowly. Home was at One Hundred Thirty Third Street, Manhattan! We were worlds from there! With only a half hour left before sailing, I was besides myself worrying, trying to figure out how to solve this dilemma. Finally, we ran to one of the ship's officers. He ran up the gangplank to the Captain. "They'll lose six months work, if they miss this ship."

While we stood rooted, the Captain lit his pipe. Then what seem like forever, but was only a second, "Well...I'll hold it for an hour."

Shirley Faye's husband flew away. Again it was thank goodness for the new subway. He was back with those tickets ten minutes before the scheduled sailing time.

The gangplank pulled up; whistles blew; great roaring and creaking, and the ship cast off from its moorings out into midstream...cheers from the dock...and the carefree "Four Creole Belles" started to Europe!

There I stood, a twenty-two year old colored girl, born of a woman who took in washing, going to Europe. Going to a new - not even imaginable life, with only two dresses to my back, not a penny in my pocket, and my hand clutched around a six months' contract, which meant hope - perhaps fame and fortune - enough to study voice on.

Thinking of studying, Momma came into my head. I hadn't written telling her I was sailing. I hadn't had the time. I didn't have the money to telegraph her. I promised myself that I'd write to her, just as soon as the ship was out of the harbour. She'd sure be proud...and as for George Mickey - well.

I looked at the always-secret buildings of Manhattan,

getting smaller, and thought of the girl, who had viewed them, with so much delight and anticipation, a year and a half ago. That girl hadn't known what it was all about. Life had only smacked her on the head, not deep down inside her. This girl sailing to dreams had pretty well learned how to score. It was glamorous, shabby, wonderful, heartbreaking, beautiful, shoddy, surprising, and you paid for everything you got - but I loved it!

I knew, too, I had more hopes, determination, more plans than ever before, youth on my side, "The Creole Belles," and with tons of personality in my favour, I couldn't do anything, but win big time.

I leaned against one of the sturdy post of the S.S. Princess Alice of the North Deutscher-Lloyd Line until I couldn't see one living thing, but water. Then I was overcome with such a wondering of what was really waiting for me. I couldn't speak anything, but English. I didn't know a soul in Europe. Yet, it was going to be the most glorious adventure. The gypsy had told me way back at that barbecue – "You will take a ship. You will travel for years by land and sea. There is a fine life to be lived." - and whether she meant it or not, I did. And if hard work, and prayers meant anything, it was all going to come true!

Printed in the United States
750300005B